The Eldermaid

K. Henderson

PROLOGUE

It is said of our world that once, all things were in balance. Holy Ilisith, God of Love, did not quarrel with Great Menaishe, Goddess of War and Maker of Weapons. Kinarshe, Ruler of Nature, Who-Was-Once-Two-But-Now-is-One, did not trade harsh words with Sudrask, He who loves Learning and upholds the Law. As for Yemena, Goddess of Death, She has always stood apart from the Others, for Death does not take sides in any quarrel.

No one is certain which of the Powers first conceived of the idea—though most would say that it was Ilisith and the followers of Ilisith blame Sudrask--but one of the Powers proposed that They join Their Gifts together in one Being as a sign of friendship and trust between Them, and so They gave this Being a part of Themselves: Courage and blood from Menaishe, Desire and flesh from Ilisith, Intelligence and breath from Sudrask, Industriousness and bone from Kinarshe, and from Yemena, the greatest of Gifts: Mortality, so that the Last Being would be ever humble in the presence of the Powers, who are Eternal.

But as the first humans—called such because they trod upon the Earth and gained their sustenance from it--grew and multiplied, the Powers found Themselves at odds with one another. Ilisith, Who hates War and strife, complained when they took up weapons to slaughter one another. Menaishe argued that without weapons, they would become powerless against others of their kind, who loved War above all things. Kinarshe was exasperated by their constant thirst for Knowledge, ignoring the welfare of the Natural World in their zeal to acquire it, while Sudrask argued that without Knowledge, they remained static, inflexible, and intolerant of those of their kind who were different. So it was, that, for a long time, warriors were barred from the Path of Love, and artists from the Path of War, farmers and merchants could not walk the Path of Knowledge, and scholars could not walk the Path of Nature. Thus was the world thrown out of balance.

And it came to pass, that while the other Powers quarreled, Smiling Yemena heard the cries of the soldier, when they said "Alas, I am without Love, for War is a harsh mistress, and taxing on the mind and body," and the artist, when they cried "I have too much Love, and cannot defend myself without knowing something of War!" and the farmer and merchant, who said "Without Knowledge, we cannot invent, we cannot innovate," and the scholar, who said "Knowledge is useless without the bounty that Nature provides, if I cannot feed myself and my children, how am I to think?!" Yemena heard them all and felt compassion for their plight, and so She called all the Powers together, and told Them of humanity's troubles, and said: "Can You not create Harmony amongst Yourselves, as You did before You created humanity?"

At her words, the Powers were ashamed that They had allowed enmity to grow among Them, and so They retired to Their dwellings to think on what could be done.

At last, Menaishe approached Ilisith, bearing a necklace in

Her hands, and She said: "I am a Smith as well as a Warrior, and see? The forge produces weapons of War and things of beauty, in service to Love. We are not so different. Should Your people show Courage above all things, they may walk the Path of War."

And Ilisith, God of Love, presented Her with a whip, and said. "Love can take many forms. See? How an instrument of War and punishment may be used in service of Love? I can be harsh, just as You. We are not so different. Should Your people revel in Desire, and possess a willingness to lay down Their weapons, they may walk the Path of Love."

At the same time Menaishe and Ilisith were coming to an agreement, Kinarshe met with Sudrask, and Sudrask said "I thirst for Knowledge, but I am also a Teacher. If I taught Our people to respect Nature, would You give them food to eat and clothes to keep them warm? Could We come to an understanding?" and Kinarshe replied. "If You would teach them to respect Nature, I would give them food to eat and clothes to keep them warm, and nurture the Knowledge that brings understanding of all who live in the world, for without Knowledge, people are inflexible, and without Nature, they starve and suffer."

And Sudrask said "So long as Your people display Intelligence, they may walk the Path of Knowledge."

Kinarshe replied "So long as Your people show Industriousness, they may walk the Path of Nature."

And so the Powers were once again in accord, and humanity prospered under Their guidance. Then one day They came together, and said "Humanity grows too dependent on Us, they grow complacent, and are not able to grow. We should withdraw for a time, and give them a chance to grow and change," and since They found that They were all in agreement in this matter, They withdrew from the affairs of the world, all except Yemena, because Death is never more than a breath away.

Before They withdrew, however, They each gave of a fraction of Their power to create many spirits, who watch over the land and, occasionally, share their power with chosen humans.

CHAPTER ONE

I was born into this world; a world inhabited by many spirits and bereft of the Powers that made it.

It is practically impossible to live one's life having never seen a spirit; one does not believe in spirits, just as one does not believe in the sky or trees or rocks, they simply *are*, and it is the dream of many that a spirit will find them worthy enough to bond with them, for the spirits choose us, not the other way around, *never* the other way around.

I was one of those dreamers, having grown up listening to the tale of how my mother met her Ember while the flamemaid crouched in the hearth, smiling wryly, though she had heard the same tale a thousand times before.

"And once the ember rested under my skin, we were truly joined together," said my mother, grinning at the spirit. Ember snorted. "You make it sound so poetic, my Augusta, as I recall, you demonstrated the full extent of your colourful military vocabulary, I believe you said—"

My mother held up a hand to stifle any further comment from the spirit. "Someday Hedda will be of age for that sort of

language, my dear, but, ah, perhaps that is a story for another time. Ah, speaking of which," she rose from her seat, beckoning for me to follow her. "Time for bed, Hedda."
I groaned, it was not yet sunset, still early, and I liked listening to my mother tell stories of when she was in the army, fighting alongside Ember, for flamemaids were a welcome addition to any fighting force, but I rose—very reluctantly, I might add—said goodnight to the spirit in the hearth, and followed my mother to my room.

"Mother, will I ever bond with a spirit?" I asked as my mother tucked me into bed. My room was beside hers. Ember often slept there in the hearth. Most spirits enjoyed sleeping close to some of their native element, but some were more adaptable than others, and Ember could technically flourish anywhere that air was present, which was, I imagined, anywhere on the surface of the world.

"I don't know, sweetheart." Mother replied, pressing a kiss to my forehead as she tucked me in. "That's up to the spirit, perhaps, if you are a brave girl, one will choose you one day."

I knew, of course, that one did not have to be brave to be chosen by a spirit, but my mother's bravery was what had drawn Ember to bond with her, so she was clearly biased in that regard, and to argue the point with her would have been folly, as a woman like my mother was seldom one to concede victory to anyone, in war or in words.

Mother paused in the doorway on her way out of my room.

"Goodnight, my Hedda," she said.

"Goodnight, mother," I replied, and then she was gone, and I was in darkness, save for the moonlight shining through my window.

I slept, and my dreams were filled with spirits.

**

There was a spirit in our elder tree.

The elder tree was just outside my window. It was the first thing I saw when I rose in the morning. That morning, there was something different about the tree, namely that there was a woman sitting in it. I knew she was not really a woman, of course, but a treemaid, an eldermaid, to be exact.

For one thing, she was green from head to toe, and naked (spirits have no need of clothing) and I did not think naked women made a habit of climbing trees. I certainly did not know of any women who had green leaves with clusters of white elderflowers from their heads. No, there was simply no possible way she could be anything but a spirit, unless she was a woman in a very elaborate costume, but I was certain it was not a festival day, and I had never heard of a festival day where women went around dressed as treemaids.

She had not looked my way yet, so I ran to mother's room, almost crashing headlong into the closed door in my haste.

"Mother! Mother!" I exclaimed. "There is a treemaid in the elder tree!"

My mother was just adjusting the dark red jacket of her Officer's uniform, which she wore proudly, even on days that were not festival days.

From her bed of coals, Ember flared up angrily.

"A maid? In my elder tree?" She exclaimed, snorting like an angry bull ready to charge, and I fought the urge not to laugh at her indignant expression. All spirits are territorial to some degree, maids more than knights, but less so than jacks; with bonded spirits being more ferociously territorial in general.

My mother frowned. "No, Ember, I'll not have you burn down the house on account of one treemaid. Go and rest in the hearth while I go and greet her with Hedda."

The flamemaid flared up again, her flames almost reaching the ceiling. "I'll not stay in here while you go to greet an interloper into my territory, Augusta!"

My mother sighed. "Very well," she said, already retrieving her thin sword in its scabbard from the cabinet in her room, but she did not draw it, merely hung it at her side. "It is usually considered rude to be armed in the presence of the spirits," she had explained to me once. "But it is always prudent to have a sheathed sword at one's side—just in case—especially when a spirit comes close to the house. Always be polite, though, my Hedda. It would not do to anger a spirit who might otherwise be a friend."

My mother only paused to fetch a flask of water, and then, with Ember and I in tow, we headed out to greet the treemaid.

The treemaid watched us as we approached the elder tree, particularly Ember, who had calmed enough that she was not flaring up or smoking or flinging sparks all over the place, always a concern with fire spirits of any kind. She floated close to my mother's side, but I could tell by the tense way in which she held herself that she was ready to defend either of us to the death if it came to that.

My mother, on the other hand, was very relaxed as she hailed the spirit:

"Greetings to you!" She called. "From whence do you

come, Lady?"

The treemaid did not answer her, instead, her gaze rested on me. She had such intense eyes, light brown like the bark of the tree she rested in. I bit my lip but managed to meet her gaze. Beside my mother, Ember began spitting sparks. My mother glared at her, and she calmed somewhat, though her expression was still one of barely suppressed anger.

"What is your name, child?" She asked.

"H-Hedda, Lady," I answered, glancing at my mother for reassurance, but she was so focused on the spirit that she did not even glance in my direction.

"Hedda," the treemaid echoed, making the sort of face that one made upon trying an unfamiliar food for the first time, as if my name had a flavor to which she had to become accustomed. Her voice was deep and musical. She sounded as if she were much older than Ember, though with spirits, you could never tell their age from listening to their voices. She could have been born yesterday, for all I knew. Actually, I did not know anything about how spirits made more spirits (assuming it was possible to make more spirits), only that there seemed to be a great number of them, more than the stars in the sky.

"Hedda," she repeated, and her expression became thoughtful. "'Battle, warrior,' an interesting name." She indicated the flask with the barest motion of her head. "Is that a gift for me, little warrior?"

"Um...." I glanced at my mother, but she was already uncorking the bottle and pouring it into the silver flask. "Take it to her, Hedda," she said, holding it out to me.

"Augusta—" Ember interjected. "Are you sure you want her near that—her?"

"It's fine, Ember," she replied. "It's past time Hedda

learned to interact with spirits other than yourself."

I took the flask from her and, holding it with both hands, walked towards the tree. The treemaid slid from her perch on one of the lower branches, landing softly and silently on the grass. She was tall, taller than Ember, even, and Ember was a head taller than mother when she decided to rest her feet on the ground. In the few years of my young life that I could remember, I could never recall feeling as small and insignificant as I did now.

She calmly extended a hand for the flask. Moss covered her fingernails, or perhaps her fingernails were made of moss, but when I went to hand her the flask, her hand drew back slightly.

"The proper thing to say before giving anything to one of my kind," she said slowly, "is 'a gift for a gift'".

I bit my lip. "A gift for a gift, just like that?"

"Just so," she confirmed, smiling approvingly at the way her new pupil grasped such things so quickly. I couldn't help but return her smile, and, although I could not see her face, I practically felt Ember scowling behind me.

"Well, then, let's try this again," I said, once again offering the flask to the treemaid. "A gift for a gift," I said, hoping I had said it with the proper sense of formality. I knew from speaking to Ember that spirits valued politeness, and sometimes their version of politeness was different from ours. She plucked the flask from my hands and drank, handing it back to me when she was finished. As Ember had explained to me once, spirits did not need food and drink for nourishment as humans did, but appreciated offerings of foodstuffs.

"A gift demands a gift in return," said the spirit. "You may call me Root, little warrior, that is the name that I am to be called among your kind." She grasped the closest branch of the tree, easily pulling herself up, and leaned against the trunk, reclining like the confident ruler of her own domain.

Ember spat sparks angrily. "You cannot be here, eldermaid!" She cried. "You will spread poison and death with every step you take upon this land!"

From her perch, the treemaid—Root—rolled her eyes. "This tree has already accepted my blood. It is a part of me, now, flamemaid, would you harm a fellow maid who has offered you no insult in a open defiance of the Custom we all hold dear?"

Ember fell silent, and my mother sighed in relief, but smiled up at the treemaid.

"You are welcome to stay as long as you wish, of course. Ember"—and here she glared at the spirit—"will learn to tolerate your presence on this land, so long as you mean no harm to its residents."

"I will not harm any who live on this land, I swear it," the spirit vowed solemnly. "And I would greatly enjoy some more of that water. Hedda may bring it to me."

"If you like," said mother, inclining her head slightly to the spirit nestled in the tree's branches. "Come along now, Hedda; we should be preparing for the evening meal, and the vegetables won't chop themselves!"

CHAPTER TWO

I brought water to Root every other day, and every day, she taught me something about the elder tree, not just how all parts of the tree were poisonous, save for the berries when cooked, or the flowers—my mother had warned me to not play near the tree as soon as I could understand speech—but how other spirits could not abide being in the presence of an elder tree.

"Not all spirits are good, Hedda," the eldermaid told me one day, and I wondered—not for the first time—where she had been before she had taken up residence in our tree, and how she had even managed to bind herself to our tree. If her birth tree had been cut down, how was it that she had survived its destruction? Every time I asked her, though; all she would do was look away and say "That is not for you to know…." and I had no wish to anger her.   I had a feeling Ember would not have approved of our frequent meetings at the elder tree, but Root had given us her vow, and I found I trusted her for all of Ember's fussing and fuming.

One night, my mother met with Root at the foot of the tree. I could hear that they were talking, but even though the tree was right outside my window, I could not hear what they were saying. Neither of them seemed angry, though, which was a relief, knowing how much Ember disliked having Root in her territory. Well, I suppose it was probably Root's territory now, too, but I did not want to be the one to tell Ember that. The flamemaid had chosen to pretend Root did not exist for the most part, and Root seemed content with that arrangement.

I had no idea how my mother was able to meet with Root without Ember skulking about (for I could not hear the flamemaid's voice) so that meant that either the subject of their talk was so unimportant that Ember did not think it worth her notice, or the talk was so important that mother had endeavored to conceal where she was going from her bondmate, something I had not thought was possible.

As I was about to give up hope of ever hearing even a little of their conversation, I heard my mother say "We'll see what Hedda says," and Root's reply of "Of course, as it has always been…."

They were talking about me! I wondered if perhaps Root had wished to speak to my mother of the things she had been teaching me. No, no, of course not! My mother already knew that Root had taken me on as her pupil of sorts, so it had to be….

I refused to believe it at first! *The bond! They're discussing the bond!* There was no way I could sleep now, I was too excited. What else could they be talking about, if not that? Yes, I was sure that was it! My mind raced, imagining how the bonding would go. Would it hurt? Mother's bonding seemed like it had been painful, but surely my mother would not have agreed to it if it meant that I would be harmed in any way.

Root was talking about bonding with me! I wanted to dance around my room, but of course, I did not want my mother to hear me and know that I knew she had been talking with Root. I was too excited to sleep now. I lay in bed, trying to imagine how the bonding would take place, seeing myself traveling with Root as we went on countless adventures, of course, I told myself I would act surprised when the time came. Mother and Root would know that I had overheard them talking if I did not act surprised.

In the end, I was surprised, but not in the way that I had imagined.

The next morning, I could barely contain my excitement when my mother called me over to the elder tree. I forced myself to walk calmly out the door to the back where the tree sat, where I was certain Root would be, and we—
--There were two treemaids in the elder tree!

The new treemaid was Root in miniature but for her eyes, which were a deep grey. She sat close to Root, feet dangling over the edge of the branch. Mother was there as well, Ember by her side, the flamemaid wearing an expression on her face which I could not read, but guessed that she was even less pleased with the newcomer than she had been with Root. Before I could open my mouth to express my confusion—and thus reveal that I had listened in on my mother's conversation, Root spoke:

"Hedda, I would like you to meet my daughter, Leaf," she said, wrapping a protective arm around the younger treemaid. "She has expressed an interest in bonding with you."

"B-B-But!" I stammered. "I thought you would—I didn't think—I thought you were going to bond with me!" At this point, I did not care if either Root or my mother knew of my eavesdropping; I wanted an explanation for this strange situation.

Root chuckled. "Ah, is that what you thought?" She shook her head. "No, child, I am not able to bond with a human any longer."

"But why?"

Root smiled. "I cannot bond with you because I am now bonded to the land itself."

My mother seemed to have made some sort of sense out of her words. "What happened to your birth tree?" She asked. Root let out a great sigh. "I was the eldest of my brethren, when my mother went back to the land, I stayed with her tree—my tree, but…. She looked down at her hands. "Now it is….gone."

Now, even Ember was attentive to the treemaid. "How did you survive, without your tree, I mean? I was unaware treemaids could survive without their tree."

In response, Root presented the back of her hand to us. "They did not destroy the whole tree…."

Instead of verdant green, the back of her hand was purple and pockmarked, like a wound that was festering.

"I took a part of the tree into myself," Root explained. "A splinter, only, but it was enough to keep me bound to this plane of existence."

Ember's mouth was hanging open, but mother was stroking her chin and nodding thoughtfully. I found myself wondering what mother knew of spirits that her own spirit did not, but I did not say anything.

"I sought out a new tree, as we treemaids normally do

when we mature," Root continued. "Instead of finding one, however; I found several." She rested her hand on the tree's trunk. "I spilled my blood on the ground and bound myself to all of them...."

"The trees were not already occupied?" Mother asked.

"No," said Root. "We prefer mature trees; saplings do not provide us with as much power, the way that a spark would not be of much use to you," she nodded in Ember's direction, and for once, the flamemaid did not spark as though Root had struck her, though her eyes narrowed in suspicion.

"But, why did you bind yourself to this tree if you already have the grove?" She asked. "That seems like a poor strategy to me if you were looking to expand your territory, O Queen of the Unnamed Elder Grove."

Root ignored the slight. Actually, she seemed more amused than offended. "Flamemaid, do you remember what I said when you first challenged my right to live on this land?"

Ember's eyes narrowed to slits. "You said 'This tree has already accepted my blood....'" and then her eyes widened. "You spawn of a lump of coal!" She cursed. "You meant that *she* had bound herself to our elder tree!" She gestured wildly at Leaf. "She is of *your blood*!" She flared up, and my mother threw herself away from the agitated spirit to avoid singeing her hair.

"Ember! PEACE!" Mother roared, and the flamemaid froze in place.

Root quit her branch. "Yes, I did trick you," she said evenly, taking a few steps towards the flamemaid. "Is it so unusual to want to provide for one's offspring? That is what I am doing—ensuring that Leaf never has to go through what I did."

She spun to face me, and I felt as if I was rooted to the spot by her gaze. "Even though I would prefer it if she remained with this tree, my daughter has expressed a desire to bond with you, Hedda, and I am not one to stand in the way of my children when they desire something." She glanced at her daughter, still in the tree, and Leaf returned the smile that Root gave her with a perfect copy of it.

Root turned her attention to me again. "I am sure this seems very sudden to you," she said. "But I do not have long before I must return to my grove, so a decision must be made, if not now, then soon."

"I told Root it would be fine with me, but that it was up to you, sweetheart," said my mother, smiling reassuringly at me.

"When did you decide this?!" Ember demanded.

"Last night, while you were sleeping, my dear Ember," my mother could barely hide her satisfied expression, likely pleased that she had been able to evade her bondmate.

"B-But how?!" Ember stammered. "I should have awakened when you moved, my Augusta!"

"I'll tell you later," she promised. "Right now, Hedda needs our full support."

"Well, Hedda," said Root. "What do you say to all this? Will you bond with Leaf?"

I bit my lip, looking from Root to Leaf and back to Root. When I had woken up that morning, I was certain that Root would be my bondmate, and even though Leaf was Root's daughter, I knew nothing about her. Still, my mother had given her blessing to our bond, and I trusted Root--even though she had deceived Ember to protect her daughter. I did not blame her for doing it. The flamemaid had been threatening to burn down the tree, after all.

I nodded. "I'll do it," I said. "I-If that's what you want…." I said to the spirit in the tree.

Leaf swung from her branch to the ground. She was, indeed, her mother in miniature, grinning broadly. "Of course I do, Hedda!" she exclaimed. "I would not have asked otherwise. Oh! We shall have such fun together!"

It seemed that while she was the mirror image of her mother, Leaf seemed much more animated than Root, who always seemed so calm and in control. I had to remind myself that Leaf was, at best, only a couple of weeks old, but spirits do not age as we do, and they are born with an awareness of their surroundings that human babies do not possess. Of course, I was not aware of the nuances at the time. At the time, I was content for that house and that tree to be my whole world, but people grow, and they change, and dream of other things, other places.

And sooner or later, every child grows up.
But I am getting ahead of myself now.

The words had scarcely passed my lips when Root smiled. "Good, it's not a complicated process. Here…" Her fingers flicked over the tree's surface, and suddenly she was holding something between her two fingers.

"A tiny part of my daughter's tree," she explained, taking Leaf by the hand and using the sliver of bark to prick her finger. I watched, fascinated, as yellow sap welled up in place of red blood and clung to the tiny piece of bark.

"Now it's ready for insertion," Root murmured.

I took a step back. "I-Insertion? W-Wha….what do you mean?"

Root glanced up and me and chuckled. "Oh, Hedda, it's not as bad as you fear it is! This sliver needs to be placed under your skin to cement the bond, so that you will always carry a part of her tree with you." She took a step closer to me. "Here now, give me your arm. It will only hurt for a moment. I give you my word."

I bit my lip and glanced at my mother, who smiled reassuringly. "It's okay, honey, I was scared too. Here, take my hand." She held out her hand and I grasped it, raising my arm so that Root could slide the sap-coated sliver into it.
Root had been right, it had only hurt for a moment, and now I couldn't feel it at all. There wasn't even a mark where the sliver had been—

I cried out as another person's thoughts flooded my mind, as my mind touched another. This wasn't right, there was only supposed to be one person in my head! *Hedda! Is she okay? She's in pain!*

No, no, that was all wrong! I was Hedda! How could I be thinking about myself in that way?!

I opened my eyes, and it was as if I saw the elder tree through a different set of eyes, eyes which saw the elder tree as glowing with a strange light.

"Hedda! Hedda! Listen to me!" My mother's voice--in the sort of tone that she used when she was not in the mood for an argument--cut through my confusion. "What you are hearing are Leaf's thoughts! You are seeing what she is seeing and hearing what she is hearing! It will be over in a moment, sweetheart, don't worry!"

I thought I heard Leaf cry out, or was I hearing my own voice through her ears? I sat on the ground and waited for the pounding in my head to stop. I don't know how long I sat there, but finally, the pain ebbed and I opened my eyes to see my mother kneeling at my side, Ember looking over her shoulder.

"It was like that for me, too," she said soothingly, drawing me close to her and gently stroking my hair. "Come , little warrior, you should rest, and be thankful that you didn't have to climb back down a mountain after bonding with a spirit!" She lifted me up as if I were a doll. "Leaf, you should come too. Staying close to each other would be the best thing for both of you right now."

"Augusta, I'll have you know I helped you climb back down that mountain!" I heard Ember grumble.

"Ah yes, Ember, always saving my ass, as you so eloquently put it," I could almost hear my mother's grin, and then there was only softness beneath me, and I knew that she had placed me in my bed.

"There you are, Hedda, Leaf. Both of you rest now." She kissed my cheek, I made an effort to say something to her, but all that came out was an unintelligible murmur; then I fell into a deep sleep.

CHAPTER THREE

It was dark when I awoke in my room, but the clang of pots and pans and the smell of meat cooking told me that it was time for dinner, unless it turned out that I had slept through the whole day, and mother was preparing breakfast.

As I went to slide out of bed, my foot struck something warm and soft.

"Ow!" Someone said, and I froze. There was someone else in my room! Was there something I could use as a weapon? No, no time! Would mother hear me if I yelled for her?

"Hedda?" There was a shuffling noise, and then. "It's me, Leaf! Don't you remember? Your mother said we were both to rest after the bond was made."

The day's events came rushing back to me. I could almost feel the sliver of the elder tree throbbing beneath my skin.

"I remember," I said, sitting back on the bed. "How come your thoughts aren't in my head anymore?"

Leaf didn't reply right away. "I asked Ember about it, while you were sleeping. She says it's to protect us from living in each other's heads all the time. She said it might take some getting used to, but we'll learn to control it, in time. Ember says the bond from mind to mind can be very useful at times." The door to my room opened and mother poked her head in. "I thought I heard you two. Dinner is ready. You should both have something to eat. I was ravenous after I bonded with Ember."

"As I recall, you nearly ate all the food in the barracks," Ember remarked blandly.

My mother glared at her bondmate. "We didn't have *that* much food, Ember! We're talking about the barracks, not an inn, and what little food they had was just barely fit for human consumption!"

"Hmph!" Ember scowled. "For food that was barely fit for human consumption, you ate much of it."

I came out of my bedroom and sat near the hearth, Leaf following close behind, though she did not sit close to the fire or Ember. Mother went to the pot over the heartk and began ladling out bowls of potato and bacon stew for us while Ember frolicked in the flames, drawing nourishment from the strong fire

I was more than a little surprised when all mother gave Leaf was a bowl of water.

"Mother, how come Leaf doesn't get any food?" I asked.

Mother looked up at me from where she was stirring the pot. "To a treemaid, water *is* food, Hedda, water and sunlight. So long as you have those things, Leaf will be well fed."

"Oh," I still felt a little guilty for eating this delicious stew while all Leaf had was water from our well, but when I looked up at the tree spirit, the look of pure bliss on her face made it clear that her simple fare was more than satisfactory. I wondered if it were possible for humans to ever experience that kind of pleasure. Of course, I was not yet old enough to partake of such pleasures that were reserved for grownups, though I knew of them, since all children are told of Ilisith and His many lovers, and my mother happily answered any questions I might have on the matter.

"Ilisith's Gift to us was Desire, after all," my mother remarked one day. "And a deity's Gifts aren't anything to be ashamed of, in my opinion, regardless of what the Order of Menaishe might think." As an Officer in the Royal Army, my mother served the Goddess of War but made no secret of her opinion of the goddess's savants, who were, according to her, "stuffy blowhards" who "wouldn't know what love was if it bit them on the ass".

According to her, the Savantry of Menaishe professed respect for Ilisith and His Gift in public while disparaging it in private, not because they were the sort of person who did not feel desire for anyone, but because some of them had a bizarre notion of what was proper. As there was no proof of this and no one would be stupid enough to publicly disparage a deity (even an absent one) however; those savants were allowed to work uncontested.

Being the child that I was, however, such political maneuverings seemed like things that happened in a distant land, of little concern to someone whose most pressing concern was trying to determine which apples were ripe for picking. I knew that Firehaven was our capital city and we had a Good and Wise Queen who was loved by all and sundry (although I wasn't too sure about the 'sundry' part) but the rest was the business of grownups like my mother, and while on some level I realized that someday 'grownup business' would be my business as well, I also knew that that would not be for some time.

I finished my dinner and helped wash the dishes before

going with Leaf to the elder tree. But this evening, instead of finding Root there waiting for us, we found the tree empty with no treemaid in evidence.

"Maybe she's just gone for a walk?" I suggested.
Leaf said nothing, only approached the tree and rested her hand against the trunk, closing her eyes and tilting her head to the side as if listening for something. After a moment, she opened her eyes.

"Mother has gone back to her grove," she said.

"Root is….gone?" I couldn't believe it, it seemed as if Root had always been there.

"She is Queen of the Elder Grove now, and now she is responsible for the welfare of that land, however small it may be." Leaf explained, letting out a great sigh. "I did not expect you to be gone so soon, mother…." She murmured, leaning against the trunk.

I felt tears well up and was crying before I could even think to stop them from flowing. "She can't be gone!" I exclaimed. "She just can't be gone!"

Leaf pushed away from the tree and came to me, wrapping her arms around me. "There, there, Hedda…." She murmured. "We both know this is how it must be."

"I know, but it's just not fair!" I grumbled.

"I know," Leaf replied. "I know."

There was nothing more that she needed to say.

We went back inside and told mother and Ember about Root. To my surprise, Ember actually seemed genuinely sad to see her go, though I knew that she was probably relieved that the eldermaid had returned to her own territory. I was wrapped in a blanket and bade to sit near the hearth while mother thought of a story to lift my spirits.

"Ah, here's one you haven't heard, Hedda," she said, leaning closer to the fire. "I'll tell you the one about the Rogue of Haven Hill, just outside of Firehaven."

I sat enraptured as she told the story of a jack who bound xirself to a hill just outside the capital city. Out of the three kinds of spirits, jacks are the most capricious and extremely selective when it comes to bondmates, preferring neither men nor women, but those who were both, or neither, or a myriad other combinations. The Rogue of Haven Hill delighted in playing tricks on the residents of a nearby town: switching the heads and tails around on cows, and causing ale to go sour, among other things. The mayor of the town had offered a purse of gold to anyone who could convince the Rogue to give up xir mischief-making. The task was accomplished by a blacksmith, who convinced the Rogue that there were tunnels under xir hill that contained so much gold that the smith had worn out all xir tools trying to unearth all of it.

The Rogue eagerly set to digging out the gold, but, upon discovering that the blacksmith had tricked xir, was so impressed with the cleverness of the smith that xe blessed xir with incredible luck, and from that day forward, the smith never wanted for anything, and died with a hill's worth of gold and a grand estate.

"That's supposedly how House Hilluck came to be," my mother remarked as she placed more wood into the fire. "I'm not sure I believe it, but it's a nice story, anyways."

"Have you ever been to Haven Hill, mother?" I asked. "Does a Rogue really live there?"

She shrugged. "I went up there, once, but if there was a Rogue living there, xe didn't see fit to show xirself to me." She leaned over to kiss my forehead. "Do you feel a bit better now, sweetheart?"

"A little," I admitted, looking up at her. "But, I still miss Root, mother, a lot."

"I know you do, Hedda," she said. "But you know, you have Leaf now, and Root wouldn't want either of you to be sad." She pulled me close to her, and I could feel her heart beating through her jacket. "She has to look after the land now, just as you two have to look after each other."

"I know," I said. "But it's so hard!"

My mother sighed, stroking my hair gently. "Sometimes life will be very hard, Hedda, but that's when you need to be brave and face life head on." She grinned. "I wouldn't worry too much about it, my little warrior. You are my daughter, after all, bravery is in our blood!"

"And you have me now, Hedda!" Leaf chirped. "I won't leave you to face life alone, not ever!"

I glanced up at Leaf. "I won't leave you alone either, Leaf."

"Good," said the eldermaid. "I'm glad."

My mother hugged me tight. "Don't worry Hedda," she said. "Ember and I will teach you all about the bond; you'll be well prepared to take on whatever life throws at you, as a true warrior should!"

For the next few years, mother taught me all she knew about the bond. I watched Leaf change with the seasons, watching the berries in her hair change from white to black and her hair change from green to yellow in the winter months. I grew as well, though I was not quite a woman yet.

I already knew that bondmates could sense each other's thoughts, but mother also taught me how to communicate with Leaf without speaking. Spirits naturally communicated this way, but humans needed to become used to it. Before long, Leaf and I could hold whole conversations without speaking a word—although mother told us that speaking this way in front of other people was generally considered rude.

But there were some things that she could not teach me, like the specifics of being bonded to tree spirits, and for that, mother took me to the nearby town of Ashville to meet an old herbalist named Igraine and her treemaid--an ashmaid, to be more specific. They lived in a little thatched cottage close to the edge of town. It seemed like a place from a storybook, with flowerpots on the windowsills and bundles of dried herbs carefully laid out for prospective customers to inspect. Nut, the ashmaid, looked as if she were much younger than her bondmate until you gazed into her deep brown eyes and saw wisdom gazing back at you. Leaf bowed her head respectfully as we entered her presence, and Nut acknowledged the greeting with the slightest incline of her head.

"Treemaids don't like eatin' out of wooden bowls," was the first thing Igraine told me as she smoked a long black pipe. "They don't much like any wood that isn't still attached to the tree, but they especially don't like eatin' out of wooden things. Best to feed 'em from metal containers, or a skin, if you have 'em. Have you been givin' her water?"

I nodded. "My mother told me they like water and sunlight."

"And sugar, if you can afford it. Don't know many around these parts that can, though. Come here, spirit, let old Igraine have a look at you…."

Leaf obediently approached the herbalist. Igraine squinted at her. "Damn my eyes!" She cursed. "Nut, she's an eldermaid, ain't she?"

"Indeed…." The ashmaid had a very rich voice.

Igraine scowled. "Figures! Listen girl!" and here she fixed me with a gaze that skewered me to the spot. "Poison is an elder spirit's friend. You can make a killin'—no pun intended—being a food taster for a noble type scared of their own shadow." She carefully set her pipe aside. "But I'd stay away from all that, if I was you. They might take you into the Royal Army, but they prefer more honourable types, flame spirits and metal spirits, the type that actually tell you they're goin' to kill you afore they do." She looked thoughtful, all of a sudden. "Unless they tap you to become an assassin, heard the Queen hires them at times—"

"--But I don't want to kill anyone!" I protested.

She glared at me. "Well, don't you jus' have rotten luck, then! Bondin' to an elder spirit!" She leaned closer, and I could smell the smoke on her breath. "The fact is that folks will judge you by the spirit you bond to, girl, and there ain't nothin' you can do about it."

She sat back in her chair, a satisfied smile on her face. "Unless you want to be like Igraine, makin' her own living sellin' her herbs instead of lettin' city folks play her like a violin, or you could become a savant." She picked up her pipe again and made a pointed gesture. "Any of the Orders would accept a bright young girl like you, regardless of your bond." Igraine rose from her seat, brushing down the plain smock she wore, and set the pipe down again.

"Regardless," she said. "You're going to have to learn to defend yourself out there, and it's better if I teach you now than you havin' to learn on your own." She walked past me and headed out the door, Nut following closely behind. "Come on, we can use the back area near the herb garden."

The back area was a tract of land worn down to dust and dirt from being trodden upon by humans and animals alike. A small herb garden occupied a corner near the house, and the whole thing was fenced in by a rickety old fence that looked like it would collapse at any moment.

Igraine brought us to an area that was a good piece away from both the house and the herb garden.

"Now, stay here while I fetch a teaching aid," She commanded as she disappeared around the corner.

I glanced at mother, who was leaning against the fence. "A teaching aid?"

Mother shrugged.

A moment later, Igraine came into view, Nut helping her carry the weight of a bale of hay.

"Need to get this….set up….here!" She grunted, releasing her burden, and I saw that the bale was actually shaped like a person. Well, it was actually more like half a person, with a part made up to look like a head, like the dolls we always made at harvest time.

"Do you make a habit of binding your hay bales into practice dummies?" Mother asked, grinning.

Igraine glared at her. "One has to work with what one has, an' this ain't the military!" She snapped, turning her attention to me and Leaf. "Now, pay attention to Nut! I don't want her to have to repeat this because you were too busy starin' at your feet!"

I turned to regard Nut. The ashmaid was standing a few paces away from the straw dummy. She appeared calm, all of her attention focused on the lump of straw. If it were a real person, I could see them being intimidated by that deceptive tranquility.

Igraine made the barest gesture with her hands, and the ashmaid sprang into action.

It was strange, watching the spirit go from absolute

stillness to a blur of motion. As I watched, Nut's arm lengthened, her hand disappearing as bark grew to cover it, forming a club, no, more like a spear, for it was pointed at one end.

There was a thump as the ash-spear made impact with the straw. Nut had run the dummy straight through its "throat", but as I watched, she slammed a second spear into its "chest", then withdrew both and hopped back, lithe and graceful as a hunting cat.

The dummy collapsed into a disheveled pile of straw.

"Ha!" Igraine crowed, triumphant. "Now there's a trick no one teaches you in the army!" She gestured to the ruined dummy. "Easy t'block the first blow, but by that time, y'see the second, it's too late!" She cackled gleefully as Nut endeavored to reassemble the dummy. "Now you, eldermaid! It's your turn!"

Leaf bit her lip. "I don't—know if I can do it," she said. Igraine put her hands on her hips.

"'Course you can, you're a spirit! Destroyin' your enemies should be as natural as breathin'!" Igraine exclaimed, gesturing to the dummy. "Come on now, get a move on!"

Leaf glanced nervously at me; I tried to give her a smile I thought was reassuring. "Come on, Leaf! I know you can do this!"

Leaf turned to regard the dummy, her lips set in a grim line, body taut like a bowstring about to release an arrow. She stood there for what seemed like a long time, just waiting….waiting….

Suddenly, she charged at the dummy. I watched, breath caught in my throat, biting my lip so hard I thought I'd break the skin.

I saw her charge the dummy, and then—

--Nothing.

Leaf had her fist up against the dummy's "throat" but nothing was happening. No spear had grown out of her arm. As I watched, her whole body began to shake, leaves, flowers and berries all trembling."I can't do it!" She cried as dark tears ran down her face. "Oh Hedda, I tried! I just can't do it!"

I ran to her, wrapping my arms around her.

"There, there, Leaf," I murmured. "It's only your first try, you just need to practice and you'll get better at it." Elderberry juice was running down my tunic, but I didn't care.

From where she watched off to the side, Igraine made a disapproving sound at us, but I thought I heard a genuine note of compassion in her voice when she spoke.

"Oh, now, don't be so upset."She said. "Nut has years of practice on you, leafling." She gestured for us to follow her inside again. "Come on now, I'll have none of that weeping in my yard, I'll fix everyone some tea and we'll be done for the day."

My mother had refrained from offering any comment on our first attempt, but now she joined us. "I think that was very well done," she said to Leaf, resting a comforting hand on the spirit's shoulder. "Someday, you'll look back on this day and wonder at how difficult it all seemed." She let her arm drop to her side, nodding towards the door into the cottage. "Don't worry about any of that now, though. Let's just go have some tea."

We took tea in the cottage. Igraine showed me how to pluck the elderberries from Leaf's hair to use in elderberry tea. "One thing's for certain," she said as she worked. "You'll always have fresh elderberries for tea and jam, as long as they're ripe enough. Leaf sat patiently as she picked the elderberries. She didn't appear to find the treatment annoying or painful, like when mother trimmed my hair and nails.

"There now," Igraine said as she finished picking. "You keep supplying me with fat elderberries like that, leafling, and I'll make sure you're well prepared to face whatever the world has to throw at you. There's a huge demand for spirit-picked berries in the city, they thinks it's some kind of delicacy," she snorted. "Delicacy, indeed! They just don't want to get off their asses and pick their own!"

As we humans drank our tea sweetened with honey, Leaf drank water, and Ember amused herself in the herbalist's cooking fire. When we had finished and the dishes were put away, Igraine bid us good day and extracted a promise from Leaf and I to return with more "of those fat elderberries" in exchange for what she could teach us.

As we walked home, mother remarked cheerfully "Well, I thought that went well, didn't it?"

Leaf frowned. "I couldn't strike the straw human." Ember snorted. "You should have seen me try to strike one made of wood! It burnt to ashes and the Training Master told me to use more restraint! Restraint! There's no room for restraint in human wars—"

"Ember…." my mother warned.

Ember seemed to realize that she was talking to a tree spirit, and she gave Leaf a sheepish look. "Sorry," she said. "We use wooden humans during practice…."

My mother folded her arms across her chest. "That's not what I meant," she told the spirit. "But, oh, we'll discuss it later."

The walk home was uneventful otherwise, and I spent the evening curled up by the hearth fire watching mother as she checked her sword for imperfections.

"A warrior is only as good as their weapons, Hedda," she'd always say, and tonight was no exception. I watched as she carefully wrapped it in oilcloth and set it aside. It was one of those things she always did, one of the many habits she picked up in the Royal Army, the rote repetition of the smallest tasks.

"Well?" she turned around to face me, smiling. "What shall we do now, Hedda? You're getting to be a little old for story time. "

"How about we play the Game of Spirits?" I suggested. Mother's smile broadened. "I had a feeling you would say that," she said, rising to fetch the special deck of cards that were only used for this particular game.

We played the Game of Spirits for awhile. I was getting better at it, and once when I won, I didn't think my mother was intentionally holding back. Ember and Leaf peered over our shoulders, attempting to help either of us cheat, but neither of us paid much attention to them. While cheating at cards was commonplace, cheating at the Game of Spirits was almost considered a form of sacrilege. The Savantry of Sudrask believed that the cards, when laid out in particular ways, could foretell the future, and some spent years studying them for that reason. "It seems like a lot of fuss for one card came," I remarked one day when we had finished a game.

Mother shrugged. "People are always looking to discern the Will of the Powers, whether by cards or some other method." Whether she actually believed the cards could foretell the future, though, she never did say. I wasn't sure I believed it myself. Why would the Powers make Their Will known through something as simple and everyday as a deck of cards? Then again, perhaps that was why the cards worked, because they were everyday things.

I watched as mother placed the cards in their special bag and stowed them away on one of the shelves closer to our bedrooms. I was tired, so we all bid each other good eve and went off to bed, Leaf settled in comfortably in the elder tree, curling up on the branch nearest my bedroom window. It was not yet cold enough that she needed to move indoors, so she liked being surrounded by her native tree. As a final precaution before going to sleep, I opened the bond between us. Even though there was no place safer than a house guarded by spirits, it never hurt to leave the bond open, just in case, always just in case.

I awoke to the howling of the wind and the pounding of raindrops against the roof. Normally, I would have simply turned over and fallen back asleep, but something told me I needed to get up and see to Leaf, maybe it was the fact that I could feel Leaf's agitation through the bond, but I quickly got up and opened the window.

"Leaf! Come inside!" I yelled over the roar of the storm. "Hurry!"

Leaf was pressed up against the trunk of the elder tree, but when I called to her, she began to crawl the short distance along the branch closest to my window. She easily hopped the gap from the tree to safety and tumbled into my room, soaking wet from the rain.

"Oh, Leaf, here, let me get you a blanket," I said, rummaging through the chest at the foot of my bed, where mother kept the blankets for times just such as this. I hurriedly wrapped the shivering spirit in one and brought her to sit on the bed with me.

"Everything is….moving all around," Leaf murmured to herself, and I had to remember that she was still a young spirit and hadn't been through as many storms as I had, and none this bad. Acting on instinct, I wrapped my arms around her, pulling her close, as mother would do for me when I was scared during storms.

"It's okay, I said, I'm here for—"

I screamed as a white flash and a great cracking sound followed by a burst of pain robbed me of the words I was going to say. I had only enough time to wonder why I was in pain when Leaf ran to the window.

"Hedda! The elder tree!" She cried, pointing.

I stood up and looked out the window.

The elder tree had been split down the middle, branches splayed on either side like an acrobat stretching their limbs. It was a strange twisted thing, no longer the steadfast companion of my childhood. In seconds, it had morphed into something that was almost grotesque.

I thought Leaf might scream or cry, but she did neither of those things, just stared at the tree—her home—in stony silence.

My door was flung open abruptly and mother appeared carrying a lantern, Ember in tow.

"What happened?" She demanded. "Are both of you well?"

I shook my head. "Mother, the elder tree—it was struck by lightning!"

My mother swore and then she was gone again, shouting for Ember to keep an eye on Leaf. The flamemaid hovered close to the eldermaid; they might have been speaking together with their minds, but I was too concerned about mother to care for the breach in etiquette.

Eventually, mother returned, soaked through even though she was wearing her heavy cloak, but otherwise fine, though she would not say why she had been out for so long, other than to cryptically reply "I was out gathering wood, Hedda," when I asked. I had my suspicions, of course, but nothing I could prove.

"I think mother went to take some of the wood from the elder tree," I told Leaf when we were alone in my room once more, a cup of cider that mother had prepared in my hands. Leaf had retrieved the blanket from where it had fallen when she had dashed to the window, and now she looked at me with interest.

"But why?" She wondered. "If she had wanted a piece of the tree, why couldn't she have waited until the following morning, or taken something before that? It doesn't make sense to use it as firewood."

I shook my head. "No," I said. "Unless….the lightning has something to do with it?" I shrugged. "If it was something important, she'd tell us."

Leaf nodded but her expression remained doubtful.

"I guess you're right," she said at last, and then she lightly plucked the mug of cider from my hands. "You are getting tired," she said. "And you will spill this if you are not careful, Hedda."

I lay back on the bed. "I do feel….tired…." I admitted, yawning. "Good night, Leaf," I murmured.

"Good night, little warrior," said Leaf.

CHAPTER FOUR

The next morning the house was empty but for Leaf and I. Leaf reported that mother and Ember had gone to town to do a little shopping, and that they would be back soon, so we were not to worry. I was still becoming accustomed to the way spirits could communicate over such great distances, but distance and time were no barriers to spirit communication I broke my fast with bread and cheese and made sure to fetch Leaf some fresh water. By the time we were both finished, mother had returned from her trip to town, loaves of bread and fresh vegetables in a basket in one hand and a deer haunch in the other.

"We have reason to celebrate today!" Mother announced, setting the foodstuffs apart from the deer haunch on the low table near the hearth.

I glanced at Leaf, but she shrugged. I guessed that Ember had not informed her of this little development.

"Why are we celebrating?" I asked.

Mother grinned, and I thought I saw a mischievous glint

in her eyes. "Why, because I've made arrangements with your Uncle Lenatus for you to study at the Temple of Kinarshe in Firehaven," she sat down next to me. "Lenatus has offered to take you on as an apprentice of sorts; you will be able to learn a great many things under his guidance."

For a moment, I sat there, too stunned to speak. The very thought that I would leave this house, with its warm hearth and many memories, the house where I had grown up; the very thought was disconcerting, to say the least. All of a sudden, my childhood dreams of great adventures with Leaf became less appealing to the girl on the cusp of womanhood.

"But I have Igraine to teach me!" I protested. "Why do I have to go to Firehaven if I have her?"

My mother sighed, placing a hand on my shoulder. "Igraine can't teach you forever, sweetheart, and I think the time has come that you were exposed to a part of the world that isn't this house, talk with people your own age." She smiled reassuringly. "I'll be coming along with you, as well, so you and Leaf won't have to face this alone. I have business to take care of in the city, anyways." She grinned broadly. "Think of it as a grand adventure!"

I sighed, still uncertain. "Do you think mean it?"

Mother pulled me into a tight embrace. "You will love the city, Hedda." She stated. "It will be okay, mark my words. The city was made for a girl like you."

It took us a month to prepare for the move to Firehaven, as my mother sent and received many missives, presumably to my uncle at the temple. Some of these she read with a frown on her face. At the time, I didn't think much on it, only waited anxiously for the day when we would leave this place for our new home, and an uncle I'd never met.

Then, on the last day, just before we doused the hearth fire, mother took me aside.

"I have a surprise for you," she said, gesturing to a strange cloth-wrapped bundle. "Be careful when you open it."

I gingerly unwrapped the bundle, gazing at the treasures I found inside. One was a dagger, the hilt embossed with delicate twining vines, but the other was a strange weapon I'd never seen before, though it resembled a spear. "What's this called?" I asked, picking it up and examining the blade with interest. It was single-edged, almost like an axe, but the entire weapon more closely resembled a sword on a stick than a halberd.

"A glaive," my mother answered. "Few travel without arming themselves first, and you're old enough to handle a blade responsibly now." She ran a finger along the wooden handle. "Do you notice anything familiar about it?"

I followed her finger with my own, wondering what I was supposed to find familiar about the handle, when all of a sudden, Leaf was by my side.

"My tree!" She exclaimed, gesturing wildly at the weapons. "What have you done to my tree?!"

"It's only a part of your tree, Leaf," my mother explained calmly. To me, she added. "I incorporated some of the wood from the elder tree into the handle. There's also a piece of it embedded in the dagger's hilt. It is said that lightning-struck trees make exceptionally good weapons, so when the opportunity presented itself, I took it."

I glanced down at the weapons, then back at my mother. "If the weapons are destroyed, will Leaf be…hurt?" I asked carefully.

Mother shook her head. "Not at all, she is bound to *you* now, Hedda, not the tree, but the presence of the wood in your weapons will strengthen your connection to each other. Here…." She fastened a belt around my waist and another over my shoulder, then slid the glaive in place at my back and placed the dagger in a sheath at my side. Unused to the weight, I teetered off balance for a moment before she caught me, placing her hands on my shoulders.

"Easy now!" She laughed. "Soon they'll feel like an extension of your arm, Hedda, but until then I want you to wear them every day to get used to their weight."

I turned to Leaf, grinning. "How do I look, Leaf?" Leaf's expression was thoughtful. "I don't know how I feel about you wearing my tree…" She came around behind me, and I could feel the slightest pressure as she touched the wooden handle. "Oh!" She exclaimed. "I can still feel it!"

I frowned, puzzled. "Feel what?" I asked.

Leaf came back around to where I could see her. "It's….hard to explain…." she admitted, biting her lip a little. "I can feel the tree's….life….I suppose you could say." She broke into a wide grin. "Will you be wearing them all the time?"

"Well, I don't think I'll be wearing them to bed!" I replied, matching her grin with one of my own. "But often, I think, especially when we're in the city."

"Speaking of which," my mother said, gesturing for us to follow her. "Come, it's time to douse the hearth fire."

When everyone in our small family had gathered together, mother formally doused the hearth fire, thanking it for providing us with light, heat and warmth, and expressing our wish to be able to light a new hearth fire at our new home. "In the old days," Ember told us. "This ceremony would be accompanied by a prayer to Menaishe for protection on the journey to the new home, but all the savants say that the Powers are gone now, although many say they still listen and watch from afar."

I said a silent prayer to Menaishe anyways, on the off chance that She was listening, regardless of what the savants said. The last thing my mother took from the house was a coal from the hearth, to be added to the new hearth fire; the old nourishing the new.

Then we were finally on our way.

The remainder of our belongings that had not been sent to the city earlier that month were out front in a cart. I was still puzzled by how much there was in what seemed like such a small home, but mother didn't seem concerned at all. The cart was pulled by a team of two dark horses; mother took their reins, and I slid into the seat next to her. Ember floated alongside the cart. close to my mother, and Leaf had claimed a place inside it. She looked like a motley collection of leaves and berries to any passersby, but mother assured me that the citizens of Firehaven were used to having spirits around them, so there was no need to conceal her.

The very thought that I would need to conceal the eldermaid was puzzling to me, as spirits had been as much a part of my world as the hearth fire. I thought about questioning mother further, but before I could open my mouth to say something, she snapped the reins, and I turned to glance back at the house where I had spent my childhood for one last time before focusing on the horizon, towards my future in an unfamiliar city.

The journey to Firehaven, mother informed us, would take a few days worth of travel, but that there were plenty of inns along the way. That night, we stopped at one such inn. The innkeeper, an older man who was balding, didn't even glance at the two spirits we had with us, merely handed my mother a key for a room and directed us to the common room, where we could have a hot meal. I sat with Leaf and Ember at one of the low tables in the common room while mother went to find some food for us.

There were a few other people in the room: a man carrying a lyre that I assumed was a musician of some sort, two finely-dressed women who didn't seem as if they were dressed for a long journey, talking quietly with their heads close together, and, perhaps most intriguing of all, a golden-haired man with a sword at his back. He looked like a warrior to me, though he was not dressed in a uniform like my mother wore. But what I found most interesting about him was not that he carried a sword, but the treeknight that hovered near him. I knew he was a knight by the way his body was formed of sharp angles, making him seem more like a living shield than a spirit, a form which made them ideal for fortifying walls and siege engines. It was said that it was next to impossible to break through a barrier that a knight placed around his bondmate, and they were sought by armies and guard companies for that very reason, though they lacked the pure offensive capabilities of maids and were the most placid of the three known types of spirits, but of course, just because they were placid did not mean they weren't dangerous. This knight's features were hidden by greenery so that only his mouth was exposed. *What an odd part to leave uncovered.* I thought as I watched them. I had never seen a knight up close before, but then the knight turned his head towards me, and greenery grew to cover his mouth the way a person would slide a visor down on a helmet and he took up a defensive position near his bondmate. And then I saw that the object of his attention was Leaf, who had decided to approach him while I was not looking.

"Hello, Brother," she greeted him, holding out both hands in front of her, palms up in a gesture that was likely meant to appear non-threatening.

Powers! I swore as I swung my legs over the bench, practically leaping out of my seat as I ran towards Leaf.

"Leaf, no!" I shouted.

Just as I thought that the knight was going to hurt Leaf in some way, the man rested a hand on the spirit's shoulder.

"It's fine, Seed. She just wants to say hello." He nodded to me. "Is this your treemaid, girl?"

I halted in mid-dash. "Yes, ser, she is."

He laughed. "Don't call me 'ser', Powers! It makes me feel so old! Call me Kainet, and the over-protective knight here is Seed." He jerked his thumb at the knight, then leaned in close to me. "He doesn't like being called 'over-protective' though, he's 'merely looking out for my safety'," he whispered, grinning impishly.

"My name is Hedda, and this is Leaf," I said, suddenly finding myself looking down at the floor. I didn't have a lot of experience talking to people who weren't my mother, and for once, I found myself unable to find the words I wanted to say. "I'm…sorry Leaf startled you," I said to Seed, hesitantly glancing up at the spirit. I found it disconcerting how the foliage hid most of his features, but Leaf seemed rather intrigued with the knight, and I supposed that she would, quite possibly having never laid eyes on one before.

The knight turned to regard me, and I tried not to flinch under the weight of his gaze.

"It's….fine…." He rumbled slowly, like he was weighing

the impact each word would have before he said it.

Kainet grinned. "Seed doesn't talk much, but then, no knight ever does." He patted the spirit's shoulder. "That's about as much as you'll get out of him in an entire conversation, , but I don't mind it much, I like the quiet, and he's a great listener, when you need one." He sat down in his seat, gesturing for me to join him, but I shook my head.

"I really should be watching our table," I said. "Mother wouldn't like it if someone else took our spot."

"Suit yourself," Kainet shrugged, but relaxed in his seat, pointing at Leaf with his chin. "I haven't seen very many bonded in this part of the country. Where are you headed?"

It seemed like an innocent question, so I was quick to reply. "We're headed to Firehaven," I said.

Kainet nodded. "I'm heading in that direction as well, there's lots of work there for--" he coughed "—for anyone who wants to make a fresh start."

I didn't miss the way he faltered a bit, as if he wanted to say something else, was he a criminal of some sort, fleeing from the law? I thought about asking him about it when mother came into view. "Hedda! Would you like some foo—"

She paused in mid stride, staring at Kainet. Kainet gazed back at her, his expression neutral. "Evening, ma'am," he said, making a hat-tipping gesture.

My mother scowled; an expression she rarely wore around me. "Hedda, come away, now!" She ordered, moving to my side in the space of a heartbeat. Beside her, Ember sparked in alarm.

Kainet simply sat in his seat, keeping his expression politely neutral.

My mother herded me back to our table, where two bowls of soup, a loaf of crusty bread, and a bowl of water were waiting for us. I started to turn in my seat to see where the man had gone, but my mother snapped "Don't look at him, Hedda," and that was that.

"But why?" I asked, confused. "He wasn't hurting either of us, mother, just making conversation."
My mother sighed, rubbing her temples. "His kind don't just make conversation," she muttered, looking me in the eye. "Just….stay away from him."

I ate my soup in silence. It was delicious, beef stock and onions with cheese on top, and the bread was still warm. In fact, the only thing that was unusual about the evening was how my mother had acted around Kainet. Did she know him from somewhere, and, if so, when, and where? Did she know him from her time with the Royal Army? Mother was focusing on the bowl of soup, so I stole a glance at Kainet's table. It was empty. There was no sign that he'd ever been there, and I didn't think he had just happened to grow tired of the atmosphere in the common room and left right after my mother pulled me away.

So many questions, so few answers. I thought as I took another bite of bread.

We finished eating and then went up to our room for the night. I didn't know what I was expecting, but the room seemed rather large for the size of the inn. Still, there were two beds and ample space for both spirits, even a fireplace where Ember could sleep, shielded from the rest of the room by a screen. In one room there was a shallow pan of water. I looked at it questioningly, but Leaf merely stepped into it and sighed happily.

Well, that makes sense. I thought. *Tree spirits absorbing water through their roots…feet? Feet-roots?* I didn't recall her ever doing anything of the sort at home, but then again, we had never thought to give her a shallow pan, only metal buckets, which she drank as any human would.

"Leaf, why didn't you ever tell us that you could drink through your feet?" I asked.

The eldermaid shrugged. "You never asked, Hedda."

"Oh," I said. "I guess that's true, but….you can tell me things like that, Leaf. We share a bond, right?"

Leaf's eyes had been closed throughout this whole exchange, but now she opened them.

"Always," she said firmly.

That night, while I lay in bed, I glanced toward where Leaf stood in the pan of water, her eyes shut.

"Leaf, are you awake?"

"What is it, Hedda?" She asked, turning her head this way and that way. "Do you hear something strange? Is someone trying to break into the room?"

I blinked. "What? No, Leaf, everything's fine, I was just wondering…." I bit my lip. "About Seed, do you….like him?"

There was a pause before Leaf responded. "What do you mean?"

"Well," I began. "It's just….the way you were looking at him, I thought…."

"What? Hedda, what are you talking about? I don't— Oh!" It was dark in the room, but suddenly I felt very embarrassed. No, I wasn't embarrassed, I realized, that was how Leaf felt.

"You thought that—", and then she giggled. Leaf was laughing at me! "No, Hedda, spirits don't….we don't"—she made a vague gesture—"it doesn't work the way it does with humans…."

"Oh," I felt my face flush. "I'm sorry, Leaf! I didn't mean

to—"

There was a splash as she left the pan, and then she was coming towards me, cupping my face in her hands.

"It's okay, Hedda," she said. "I don't mind answering any questions that you might have about anything, even something like spirits being together."

I was certain she could feel my cheeks heating though her hands.

"No, I….was just wondering. You seemed so fascinated by him, that's all," I remarked.

This time, I could almost see her grin. "Well, I've never seen a knight before. I know about them, of course. All spirits are born knowing of others of their kind, but whether we ever get to see them is another story."

She turned and walked back to her pan. "Now, we both should get some rest, Hedda. It's still a ways yet to Firehaven, judging by what your mother said."

I started to open my mouth to reply but all that came out was a yawn.

"I'll see you….in the morning, Leaf," I murmured as I rested my head against the pillow. I fell asleep before I heard her reply, and slept peacefully through the night.

We left the inn early the next morning. I looked around the common room for Kainet before we broke our fast, but he was nowhere to be seen, and I didn't think mother would appreciate my asking after him. Perhaps he had left in the night. In any case, I decided to put him out of my mind for the time being, and focus on the journey we had ahead of us. Fortunately, apart from that first night at the inn, the rest of the journey was uneventful, save for the sighting of the occasional deer. We saw few others on the road apart from a merchant wagon. Mother told me it was not that unusual to see so few on this road, as there were many more roads that were much more convenient for merchants looking to trade with the port city of Seacliff, which shipped goods all over the world. "I'd like to see the sea someday," I remarked when mother told me this.

She smiled indulgently at me. "Perhaps we could take a trip to Seacliff someday, Hedda, once we've settled into Firehaven. Nowhere else has such excellent seafood."

"Seafood?" Ember wrinkled her nose. "I'll never understand why you humans like to eat some of the things that you eat."

"No," said my mother, grinning impishly. "But you don't seem to mind cooking it for us!"

I couldn't help but giggle at the way Ember scowled, and it seemed like, as short as the journey was, it could have lasted forever, so long as I had mother at my side.

CHAPTER FIVE

In a few days time, we arrived at Firehaven.

Mother woke me as the stone gates to the city came into view.

"Look, Hedda! We've arrived at last!" She could barely keep the excitement from her voice, and Ember nearly set the cart ablaze with her enthusiastic spark-spewing.

"What is going on?" Leaf asked sleepily, poking her head out from beneath the canopy.

"Leaf! We're here!" I exclaimed. "Firehaven!"

"Come up in front and see, Leaf," mother said, patting the space between us. "You only see the gates of Firehaven for the first time once in your lifetime."

Leaf scrambled over the cart to join us up front, staring up at the stone with wide eyes.

"It looks so....lifeless...." She said at last.

Mother laughed. "I wouldn't worry, Leaf!" She said. "There's plenty of greenery inside the city, especially at the Temple of Kinarshe." She nudged me, "Look," she said, pointing. "You can see images of each of the Powers carved into the gate."

It took me a moment to see them, but once I did, they were unmistakable. There was Menaishe, with Her sword and smith's hammer, Sudrask, with His books, Kinarshe, surrounded by greenery, and Ilisith, proudly naked and wearing a secretive smile.

"It is said that King Harok the First tried to remove Ilisith's carving from the gate," mother remarked. "He was fanatically devoted to Menaishe, and thought a city dedicated to War did not need Love. After he died—after Ilisith Himself killed him—it is said He miraculously restored His image to its rightful place on the gates, and so it remains. No one dares attempt to alter the images of the Powers, now. If you ask me, it was stupid of Harok to try in the first place."

I glanced up at the gates, noticing that one deity was unaccounted for.

"What about Yemena?"I asked. "Why is there no carving of the Lady of the Dead?"

Mother smiled. "That is because Death is always with us. We do not need to be reminded of Her presence with images in stone, for She is always there. We should visit her Grove in Firehaven, actually." She said thoughtfully. "It would be very instructive."

We were actually passing through the gates, now, if I looked straight up, I could see the watchtowers where the guards were always on the lookout for threats from outside the city.

And then we were in the city proper, and I forgot all about the gates and kings and Death.

I had never seen so many people in one place before, and they were all moving in different directions, headed for Powers-knew-where. Our cart had to stop every few paces so that they could pass.

"Look, mother! Look!" I cried, as if I were half my age again, pointing at a merchant hawking cider at a little stall. It seemed that there were lots of little stalls here with people selling various things.

"Ah, the Moving Market, some things never change," mother observed. "The stalls are designed to be quickly disassembled in the event of an attack on the city, or in the event that the guards become wise to your....unscrupulous endeavors...." She snapped the reins, and the horses turned westward. "Hopefully the Temple of Kinarshe is in the same place it was when I left the city, or I'm afraid we'll be quite lost!"

The road that we turned down was not lined with buildings. In fact, as we continued down the road, the number of buildings I saw became fewer and fewer until finally, only one dominated the landscape.

"Ah, here we are," mother said as she gently guided the horses to a stop in front of the building. It was a plain, squat, round building that was a warm golden colour, and if my mother had not been so certain that this was the Temple of Kinarshe, I probably would have guided the horses right past it.

As mother jumped down from the cart, the door to the temple opened, and a tall dark-skinned man in blue and green robes came forward to meet her. "Sister," he said, kissing her cheek. "Welcome back...."

"It's been a long time, brother," she replied.

The man—my uncle--smiled. "This time, I hope you'll stay, Augusta. I've missed you," he rested a hand on her shoulder, "*she's* missed you."

My mother's expression turned sour. "Now is not the time to speak of such things, Lenatus," she turned to me then, waving me over. "Hedda, come and meet your uncle!"

I slid down out of the cart and went to stand at mother's side, suddenly feeling very shy. Uncle Lenatus' smile changed to a more thoughtful look as he examined me, at last he made a "huh" sound, as if he had just figured out the solution to a difficult puzzle, and then the smile was back again.

"Well met, niece, at long last, well met," he said. "What does your mother call you?"

"Hedda, ser," I said immediately.

"Hedda," he repeated. "A good, strong name—and it's not 'ser', it's 'Uncle Lenatus' to you, young lady. Welcome to the Temple of Kinarshe." He gaze landed on Leaf. "Ah! A treemaid! Is this your bondmate, Hedda?"

"My name is Leaf, Hedda is mine and I am hers," said Leaf. "Pleased to meet you, Savant Lenatus."

Uncle Lenatus bowed deeply to her. "The pleasure is all mine, I assure you. The tree spirits who live in this temple will be delighted to have you among them, I'm certain."

I wasn't so sure about that. "I thought tree spirits were territorial," I said hesitantly.

Lenatus nodded. "Indeed, that is true for most spirits in general, but within the temple, tree spirits have co-existed in harmony for many, many centuries. Ah, Ember!" He turned to the flamemaid, a grin on his face and a mischievous glint in his eye. "Take care not to burn the temple down, eh?"

"Me? I wouldn't dream of it!" Ember replied, and Lenatus laughed, a deep, rich sound that couldn't help but bring a smile to my face.

"Come," said Uncle Lenatus, gesturing for us to follow him. "I'll show you to your rooms."

The room Uncle Lenatus had set aside for us was sparsely furnished with a table, two chairs, and small beds that could fit one person at the most, but, despite that, the room radiated a warm, welcoming atmosphere.

"Our new home won't be ready for a few days," mother explained as she removed her travelling boots. "The savants have graciously allowed us to stay with them until then."

She turned as the door opened and Uncle Lenatus came into the room.

"Hedda, why don't you go and find Leaf?" She suggested. "I think she's in the Inner Court with the other tree spirits. I just need to speak with your uncle for a bit."

Well, it wasn't like I had anything better to do, so I nodded and left the room, gently closing the door behind me. Taking a deep breath, I opened the bond between me and my eldermaid.

Leaf?

What is it, Hedda?

Where are you right now? Mother wanted to speak to Uncle Lenatus alone, so she suggested that I find you.

I'm in the green place at the centre of the temple. Oh! You need to see it, Hedda! It's beautiful! Where are you now?

I'm just outside the door to our rooms. I sent back.

I'll give you directions from there, then.

Following another's directions was much easier when you shared a bond of mind to mind with them, and in no time I came upon the place mother had called the Inner Court, which suddenly appeared as I turned a corner, as if conjured from the air.

I stood, slack-jawed in awe, at the sight before me.
The 'green place', indeed. I thought as I took it all in. The ground beneath my feet was a carpet of bright green grass, green ivy twined up the gigantic statue of Kinarshe, who was seated and cradling a wide array of flowers in Xir arms. At Xir feet grew fruit trees, and all around Xir, the largest trees I had ever seen stood like sentinels.

And of course, there were the tree spirits.
I watched as a group of treemaids danced in a circle while a treeknight guarded them. Treejacks flittted about without a care for anyone or anything in their way. There were savants there too, tending to the grounds or speaking to individual spirits, likely their bondmates, but, if what Uncle Lenatus had told me was true, I suspected that not all these spirits were bonded to humans.

"Hedda!"

I turned towards the sound of Leaf's voice to see her waving at me. "Come here!" She called. "I want to introduce you to someone!"

I obligingly walked across the grass to meet her, trying as best I could to keep out of the way of the cavorting spirits. A treejack came towards me, but, after glancing at Leaf, let out a great, high-pitched laugh and sped away, likely intent on making some mischief.

Leaf was standing by another treejack, xir skin was the color of dark cherry wood, and delicate pink and white blossoms sat atop xir head.

"Hedda, this is Flower," Leaf said. "Xe's the bondmate of the Head Savant of Kinarshe."

Flower extended a hand to me, which I took without

hesitation. "Your bondmate has told me much about you, Hedda," xe said.

I have to admit, xir manner of speaking was not what I was expecting from a treejack.

"Are you—truly a treejack?" I blurted out, instantly chastising myself inwardly the moment after the words left my lips.

Flower snorted. "Another who thinks that all jacks sow naught but chaos, I see,"

I shook my head. "Oh no, please excuse me, Ser Flower, I did not mean to imply—"

"Shh," the treejack placed a finger over my mouth. "I forgive you, child. Let this be a lesson to you: do not judge others solely based on the labels that others give them. Now…." and here xe turned to Leaf. "If you will excuse me, I have duties to attend to in this temple," and with that, xe turned and strode away, but not before turning and calling back over xir shoulder "--and I quite like being called 'Ser Flower,' I think. You will call me that again, when next we meet, child," and then xe was gone, and I was alone with Leaf.

"I wonder if mother and Uncle Lenatus are done speaking yet," I said to her. "Perhaps we should go and see." Leaf readily agreed to my proposal, so we headed back through the small maze of corridors to our room.

As we neared the room, it became clear that mother and Uncle Lenatus were arguing, and by the volume of their voices, they weren't trying to hide that fact from anyone. I motioned for Leaf to be quiet and crept towards the door, curious to hear what they had to say and wondering if this had something to do with when mother was in Firehaven last.

"I won't go back, Lenatus, I can't," mother was saying.

"Augusta, you have to go back at some point. You can't

hide here forever, what about Hed—"

There was a muffled thump. I thought it was my mother's fist slamming into the table.

"No, Lenatus," my mother was firm. "We're staying only as long as it takes to train Hedda in the same way that you train your bonded acolytes, and no longer."

"Augusta, please," Uncle Lenatus was pleading now. "At least consider it."

I heard my mother sigh, but she did not respond to my uncle.

"Fine," I heard him say, and I quickly ducked into the shadows as he opened the door and left the room, looking defeated.

I waited a few minutes so that mother would not suspect that I had heard their conversation, then knocked on the door. "Mother? I saw the Inner Court, but I'm bored now." My mother was seated at the table, head in her hands, but when I came in she looked up and smiled at me.

"Bored? In the Inner Court?" She shook her head, but her smile remained. "They must have redecorated it since I was a girl, I remember it being spectacular. In any case, if you want to go to bed, my darling, that's fine with me."

That sounded like as good an idea as any, because it now seemed like the journey was catching up to me, and I suddenly felt very, very tired. "Don't worry," Leaf assured me as I drifted off to sleep. "We'll find answers tomorrow, okay, Hedda?"

"Okay," I murmured, closing my eyes and falling into a deep sleep.

The next day, our quest to find answers was delayed by the arrival of my first moonblood. Leaf never left my side that day, hovering even as I disrobed to bathe, until mother herded her out of the bathing area, saying. "Oh, for Ilisith's sake, Leaf! She's not bleeding to death, I promise!"

One of the savants came to give me a strange concoction of herbs that she claimed would help with the pain, as well as some rags that I could use for the duration of my moontime, and then, after suggesting I rest when I was finished bathing, she left me to soak in the hot water.

I was not bothered for the rest of the day. When the worst of the pain had subsided—thanks, no doubt, to the concoction that the savants had brewed--I dressed in a simple linen nightdress and, shadowed by an anxious Leaf, returned to our suite of rooms immediately falling into bed.

I slept until that evening. The pain was just a memory by that time, but the rags between my legs were proof that it had not been a dream. Leaf watched anxiously as I swung my legs over the side of the bed. I would not have been surprised to learn that she had watched me while I slept, but she insisted that that was not the case, she had merely stood guard outside my door, only running in to check on me from time to time.

"Leaf, I'm fine," I assured her for the hundredth time as I slid my feet into a pair of sandals like the ones the savants wore. "If I were bleeding to death, don't you think I would have died by now?"

Leaf shook her head. "It's not just that, you smell different, you feel different, the bond between us feels stronger, somehow."

"It's because she's no longer a child, now," Ember interjected, striding into the room. "She's maturing physically in a way that we spirits do not. I would be more surprised if you didn't feel out of sorts at all, Leaf." To me, she said. "Are you feeling well enough to eat, Hedda?"

I nodded. "The pain is mostly gone now, and I am feeling a little hungry…."

Ember nodded. "Good, your mother was hoping to take you to the Temple of Ilisith tonight for your Making Ceremony…."

My mother had told me of the Making Ceremony, of course, for it was the point at which a person passes from child to adult, but at the time she had told me about the ceremony; it had seemed so far away that I did not think on it at all after that. Now I was as anxious as Leaf had been all day, though I did manage to eat the soup that was offered to me. After I had dressed in my best clothes, mother commandeered a carriage to take ourselves and our spirits to the Temple of Ilisith for the ceremony.

CHAPTER SIX

The Temple of Ilisith could not have been more different than the Temple of Kinarshe. Where the Temple of Kinarshe was squat, the Temple of Ilisith reached for the sky, and while the Temple of Kinarshe preferred soft lighting, even at night, the Temple of Ilisith was like a beacon in the darkness.

"The only temple that rivals this one in brilliance is the one dedicated to Menaishe, close to the Palace," mother explained as we all piled out of the carriage, gesturing for me and Leaf to go ahead of her.

"Go ahead, sweetheart," she said. "Custom dictates that you are to enter the temple first."

I looked around to get my bearings; the door was not so far away, but I was unused to being outside when it was this dark out. "Why are there no guards to watch for trouble?" I asked suddenly. The Temple of Kinarshe employed a few guards to watch over the sacred precincts, but their absence was notable here.

"Ah, that," said my mother, stepping up beside me. "The Temple of Ilisith has never employed guards, only once did they break that rule, during the time of Harok the Mad. It goes back to when those who took up weapons of War were banned from entering Ilisith's Order. That has changed now, but the custom has not."

We had reached the doors of the temple. They were large and made of stone, depicting the God of Love cavorting with His lovers. The doors had a pair of golden handles, and these I grasped and tugged.

To my surprise, the doors slid open easily, I took a breath and stepped across the threshold with Leaf hot on my heels, mother and Ember following along behind. The room we were in was lit softly by candles; the shadows of the flames dancing on the stone walls. I could smell the subtle perfume of incense and hear the soft lilting sound of a flute.

"Welcome to the Temple of Ilisith," a soft voice said, and I turned to see an older man, his hair going from silver to white, on the far side of the room. He was dressed in saffron robes, and radiated a kind of calmness and self-assurance that was typical of a savant.

"H-Hello, ser," I said. "I—ah…." I glanced at my mother for reassurance. She had not told me if I was supposed to say anything in particular.

"What my daughter is trying to say," said mother helpfully "is that she has had her first moonblood today, and wishes to undergo the Ceremony of Making."

"Ah," the old savant smiled beatifically. "Blessings to you on this momentous occasion, child! I shall return in a moment with someone who will conduct you through the ceremony.

Please, wait here a moment." He gestured to a couch just to the left of the door he had entered through, and then he hurried away to accomplish his task.

I sat down on the couch; it was plush, luxurious, a rich burgundy in colour, clearly made for comfort over functionality, and turned to mother. "Why couldn't he conduct the ceremony?" I asked.

"The ceremony can only be conducted by one who bleeds every month, Hedda," mother explained.

"Another tradition?" I asked.

"Just so," she replied, grinning.

"You humans certainly have many traditions," Leaf mused, examining an ivy plant that was set into a recess in one wall, apparently left to climb wherever it wished to. "Well, I'll say this for them, they take good care of their plants."

At that moment, the old savant returned, a young man in tow. The man had light blond hair and olive skin, and he bowed briefly to us.

"I great you in the name of Ilisith, Lord of Love," he said, gaze resting on me. "Are you the one who has come for the Ceremony of Making this night?"

I nodded. "My name is Hedda," I said. "But aren't you—aren't you a man?"

My mother chuckled, and the young savant just smiled. "I am," he assured me. "I am Savant Chesnos, but once my parents called me Chesna."

"Not all who bleed are women, Hedda," my mother said.

"Oh," I said, blushing a little. "Please excuse me, Savant Chesnos."

"It's not a problem," he assured me, his smile never wavering. "Come, I think we shall use the main shrine for this ceremony," and with that, he opened the door closest to us

61

and beckoned for all of us to follow him.

We emerged into a great chamber lit by hundreds of candles. The floor was made of tan marble and strewn about were many cushions in varying shades of red and purple. Looming over all, though, was the giant statue of the god Himself, unashamedly naked but for the golden necklace set with a massive red stone around His neck. Our oldest legends tell us that it was a gift given to Him by Menaishe. The god was smiling proudly, indicating the source of His pride—His phallus—with a gesture that could only be described as languid.

Chesnos handed me a stick of incense. "Here you are," he said. "Just walk up and place it with the others at the god's feet."

"Here," said my mother. "I'll light it for you…"

She touched the incense stick, and a spark flew from her finger and the stick began to release its fragrant smoke. Mother rarely used the bond between herself and Ember to pull on the spirit's power, but apparently this ceremony was an exception.

I held the stick in my hands and walked the length of the room towards the massive statue. There was a mound of sand with many sticks of incense sticking out of it, blackened by use. I stuck my stick among them, watching as the smoke wafted up, caressing the statue like an eager lover.

"Lord," Chesnos intoned from behind me, startling me a little with his nearness. "On this occasion of her first blood, may this young woman experience the fullness of Your Gift of Desire. May she learn to use this Gift wisely, without malice towards others. May she experience Love in its sweetness, as You have experienced Love in all its forms, and may Love sustain her when all hope is lost," and here he handed me a pair of golden shears. "Cut a lock of your hair, and feed it to

the flame," he murmured, gesturing to a brazier to my left.
I tried to snip off a portion that hopefully no one would notice
was missing, casting the length of red hair into the fire.

"See your shorn hair, symbol of your childhood,
devoured by the flames," Chesnos intoned solemnly. "So too,
is your childhood gone, and now you embrace a new life, not
as a child, but as a woman," he smiled. "Now is not a time of
mourning for the child you once were, but of celebration, for
the adult you are becoming." He raised his hands above his
head. "Go now, with Lord Ilisith's Blessing…."
I bowed to the savant and towards the statue, and then ran to
my mother, who embraced me.

"Congratulations, sweetheart!" She said, releasing me, her
eyes sparkling with mirth. "Ah, you're growing up so fast, my
darling!" She exclaimed. "Now, since we're here, we might as
well tour the entire temple, and then we should return to the
Temple of Kinarshe, where we shall celebrate this occasion
with a proper feast!"

Savant Chesnos was more than happy to give us a tour of
the temple. There was the main shrine, of course, but there
were also other areas dedicated to the different forms taken by
the God of Love in order to explore Love in its many forms.
As the Goddess of Love, Ilisith experienced love between
women, and in Xir form as the third-sex Ruler of Love, Ilisith
blessed the love of all those who see themselves as neither man
nor woman, but both, or neither, as well as love between
friends and the love one feels for one's family. The last form
He took was that of the Sadist, He of the lash and other forms
of Love that play with power, dancing between pleasure and
pain and back again. I will admit to feeling a little intimidated
by this form, bearing both whip and blade, its surface reddened
with flecks of dried blood from offerings, but Chesnos' smiled

fondly as he regarded the image, bending forward to reverently kiss the statue's feet.

"He may seem frightening at first," he said to me as he straightened. "But those forms of Love which He rules are no less sweet than any other, for He is a God of Compassion as well as Severity, always."

The last portion of the temple that was of interest to visitors, Chesnos informed us, was the wing that contained the sleeping chambers for visitors to the temple.

"At times," he explained. "People come to take solace from Ilisith's Gift. It is a Gift that is given freely by any of the Savantry of Ilisith, as decreed by the God of Love Himself, although, a savant has the option to refuse any such arrangement that is not to their liking. We also shelter those who are rejected by their families for Love's sake: those who love a person their family believes is 'beneath them', mostly, it does not happen overmuch nowadays. The Way of Love has enjoyed immense popularity among the people, but we always keep a few doors open, just in case." He paused at the end of the corridor. "And that is the end of the tour, unless you wish to see the storage rooms?" When I shook my head no, his smile broadened.

"Ah, then I must take my leave, then," he continued, giving us a proper courtly bow. "Farewell, Lady Augusta, and farewell to your daughter as well," and then, with a final nod, he disappeared through a door, leaving us alone in the hallway.

"He knew your name," I said to mother as we walked all the way back to the carriage. "You didn't tell it to him, did you?"

My mother's expression was grave. "No, I did not," she said, sighing a little before she exchanged her somber expression for a smile. "Let's just head back to the Temple of

Kinarshe, Hedda. I'm sure your Uncle Lenatus is waiting for us."

We returned the Temple of Kinarshe where we immediately proceeded to the Inner Court, where Uncle Lenatus was waiting with a bunch of acolytes in white robes next to a table laden with food. "Some of the acolytes are being inducted into the Savantry tomorrow," he explained. "So I convinced the other savants to let you have your Making Ceremony party here as well." He opened his arms and embraced me; he smelled of jasmine flowers.

"Congratulations, niece," he murmured, kissing my cheek. "Come, help yourself to the feast the savants have prepared, you too, Augusta, Ember, Leaf…."

Mother and I sat down to eat while Leaf drank water from the temple's wells with the other tree spirits and Ember gleefully jumped between the candles that were set around the table. This being the Temple of Kinarshe, they had a variety of fresh vegetables as well as many different kinds of cheeses, and bread that contained many different seeds. The temple's residents did not generally consume a lot of meat, but tonight, it seemed that they had made an exception, and had a small turkey as well as grilled fish at one end of the table, farthest away from the cavorting tree spirits, though one treejack decided to inspect it, quickly declaring it unfit for consumption by anyone.

When we had filled our bellies with what was on the table, the savants brought out a rich cake filled with raisins and topped with a sweet sauce, as well as a variety of candies. I enjoyed the cake so much that I begged Uncle Lenatus for the recipe. He laughed, promising that he would see that I was given a copy of it, and then I begged my mother to let me make it for us when we left the temple to take up residence in our new home.

"Of course, Hedda," my mother agreed, smiling indulgently. "But first, we shall have to go to market to find all the ingredients. Luckily, Firehaven has one of the best markets in all the land."

"Naturally," Uncle Lenatus agreed. "Firehaven is the capital, after all."

"Oh, yes, I know that," my mother replied, grinning at her brother. "Surely I haven't been away for so long that Firehaven has been forced to tolerate hosting an inferior market."

"I suppose you're right," said my uncle, returning her grin.

"Of course I am," my mother replied, taking a drink out of her mug, which I assumed contained some of the temple's finest beer. The savants brewed it in honor of Kinarshe, who had first used the plants in Xir domain in this way.

When we had all finished making merry, everyone, spirit and acolyte alike, helped to clean the Inner Court. An offering of incense was given before the statue of Kinarshe in closing, and then everyone said their good nights and went to their rooms. I didn't even bother to remove my clothes as I collapsed on my bed, the day's events finally catching up to me at last. Little did I know that there was much more to come that would make this day seem as carefree as the days that I had spent in the house with the elder tree.

CHAPTER SEVEN

We lingered at the temple long enough to witness the Plowing of the Fields, the ritual that always precedes an acolyte's induction to the Savantry of Kinarshe. During the ritual an acolyte was required to plow the fields until their white robes were as brown with dirt as possible. Kinarshe's Gift to humanity was Industriousness, after all, and the Plowing of the Fields served a practical purpose as well as a religious one.

I watched as the acolytes paraded into the Inner Court, proudly displaying their dirtied robes, each patiently waiting their turn as the savants gave them each a fruit plucked from the trees at the statue's feet, and then their new robes of green and blue. The cheer that arose as they were presented to the crowd that had gathered was deafening, and I enthusiastically joined in showering the new savants with flowers. The flowers would later be collected and used to create soil for the temple's herb gardens.

When the ritual had ended, Uncle Lenatus escorted us to the carriage that was waiting to take us to our new home. Mother, Leaf and I climbed into the back, while Ember hovered close to my mother in the form of a tongue of flame, far enough away so that she would not spook the horses.

When we arrived at the place we were to call home, I first thought that the driver had been given the wrong directions, and we had ended up at an important noble's house instead. The house was so large, and, by the Powers! I had never seen so many windows in my life! And yet, mother did not act as if anything was out of the ordinary, calmly disembarking from the carriage and striding towards the large oaken doors without giving the windows a second glance.

Well, if she's been to the city before, she must be used to it. I thought as Leaf and I hurried to catch up to her.

The scene within the house was one of complete chaos, people rushing two and fro on one errand or another. At the old house, we had had no need of servants, but the city was vastly different from the country, and I was to learn that servants were a necessary part of city life.

A young man who was standing apart from the chaos turned as we entered the room. He approached my mother, bowing hastily.

"Well met, Lady Augusta," he said. "As you can see, everyone is busy attempting to make the house as livable as possible." He leaned closer to her, and his voice dropped in volume.

"Begging your pardon, m'lady," he said. "We would have been ready sooner, but there were--" He glanced nervously at the door, as if afraid someone would choose that moment to walk through the door and catch him speaking of them.

My mother smiled, placing a reassuring hand on the man's shoulder. "It's fine, Sebastian, I understand the need for….discretion….all of the staff have done excellent work." She nodded in my direction. "This is my daughter, Hedda." She said. "You would probably not remember her, but your father would."

Sebastian peered at me. "I do see the resemblance," he said finally, holding out a hand for me to shake. "Well met, Lady Hedda."

I could not help but giggle at the use of the title. "Just Hedda is fine, Ser Sebastian," I said.

Sebastian grinned. "And just Sebastian is fine, Hedda."

"Sebastian will be our butler," mother explained. "His father held the position before him. How is Goderick faring?" Sebastian grinned. "Well enough, but cranky these days, I practically have to restrain him from trying to reorganize the wine cellar, but he has faithfully kept the manor's accounts for you, my lady, it gives him something to do."

Mother nodded. "Very good then, I'm sure having other occupants in this house besides the servants will go a long way towards keeping him busy." She grinned at him, gesturing for me to follow her. "Carry on then, Sebastian, I need to get Hedda settled in her own room."

"Of course, my lady," came the reply, and then Sebastian bowed to my mother again and went back to calling orders to the servants.

"He's a nice young man," my mother remarked as we turned a corner, moving towards a set of stairs. "I need you to be on your best behavior with all the servants, Hedda. They are as much a part of the family as Leaf or Ember."

"But then," I bit my lip. "Why didn't they come with us when you left the city?"

My mother sighed. "It's a….complicated matter….Hedda," she said at last, smiling a little.

It was starting to seem as if everything involving my mother was a "complicated matter". Once again, I had so many questions, and so few answers.

Leaf, I'd sure like to know the details behind these 'complicated matters,' I sent.

Agreed, Leaf sent back. *I'm curious to know too. Is it odd, do you think; that a spirit would be curious to know of such things?*

I don't think it's odd, I replied.

At that point, mother had stopped before a door that I assumed was my room. "Here you are, Hedda," she was saying. "My room is just down the hall, if you need me. I'll leave you two to explore a bit. If you get lost, ask the servants for help or have Leaf call to Ember," she grinned. "See if you can find all the secret passageways in the house. I don't think I ever managed to find them all."

"There are secret passageways in this house?" I asked.

"Oh yes," mother replied. "Most of the larger dwellings do, both to give the servants an easy way to move around or to provide an escape route in the event of an attack. It's always good to have some knowledge of them, just in case." She kissed the top of my head affectionately, and then headed down the hall. "Now, I really should start filling out some paperwork. Enjoy yourselves, and remember what I said about being polite to the servants!"

"Of course, mother," I murmured as she disappeared into one of the rooms and shut the door.

When I was certain we were alone, I looked up at Leaf, grinning. "Well, Leaf," I said. "I guess we have the rest of the day to find some answers!"

In actuality, I didn't find the barest hint of an answer until late that night, but I am getting ahead of myself again.

Leaf and I spent a fair amount of time just exploring the room we would share, which was at least twice as big as the room that we had shared in the old house. All of my belongings had been carefully arranged in the room, including the case for my glaive and dagger--which I always kept on me except when I was sleeping anyways--which rested at the foot of my bed. Leaf seemed to be very pleased with her portion of the room, which included a pan of water which was made of clay and decorated with images of trees. There was also a large window facing east so that she could bask in the early morning sunlight.

"Hedda, does this all seem like a dream to you?" Leaf asked suddenly.

I shook my head. "I-I don't know," I admitted. "It all seems so…." and then I realized what she had said, and my eyes widened. "Hold a moment, spirits dream?"
Leaf giggled but she didn't seem annoyed by my change of subject. "Of course we dream! You've never used the bond to see into my dreams, Hedda?"

"I didn't know it could be used in that way," I admitted. "What do spirits dream about?"

Leaf considered the question for a long moment before responding. "It is hard to put into words," she said at last "but I see and hear my fellow treemaids, and they see and hear me and we are all together for a moment." She made a vague circular gesture, as if trying to express it in words was too difficult.

She was right, I didn't quite understand all of what she

meant, but then again, ultimately spirits were not like humans, even though many of them resembled humans in shape. Then, suddenly, the realization hit me.

"You've seen my dreams?!" I exclaimed, feeling my cheeks blush hotly.

Leaf shrugged. "Once or twice," she admitted. "But they were eating dreams and playing dreams, like the one where you dreamed that Augusta bought you a puppy."

"Leaf!" I cried, blushing hotly. "I don't like when you see my dreams like that! They could be….personal….one day."

Leaf seemed to realize what I meant, and she frowned. "Of course, Hedda, but you know you can trust me to keep your secrets. We are bondmates, after all, and if you cannot trust your bondmate to keep a secret, you can trust no one in this world," and with that, she grasped my hands, suddenly excited.

"Come on," she said. "We should explore the house a bit before there's no more light left. I wouldn't want to get lost in this place in the dark!"

We spent some time exploring the house, but to our great disappointment, we found neither secret passageways nor answers, not even a stray scrap of parchment that would give us a clue as to why mother had been acting so strangely since coming to Firehaven. Defeated, we sought out Ember and mother, and together--I doing the honours with Ember's help--we kindled the fire in the house's hearth, adding the coal from the old house to it, and then we all sat down for our first meal as a family in our new home.

That night, we had the most unusual visitor.

Everyone was gathered around the hearth fire. Mother was reading a book in one of the comfortable armchairs, while

Ember basked in the flames. I sat on the floor close to the hearth, watching the flames leap and dance while Leaf maintained a respectful distance from the fire. It was raining outside, the raindrops beating out a staccato rhythm on the room.

Suddenly, there was a knock at the door; the sound seemed to reverberate throughout the house. Mother frowned, but rose to answer it, waving Sebastian away. Ember flared up suddenly, alert and at my mother's side in an instant.

The person standing at the threshold was wearing a dark heavy cloak, hood pulled up to hide most of their features. As I watched, the visitor lifted the hood, revealing a brown-skinned woman with dark hair and eyes, and full red lips. At the sight of her, Ember sighed with relief and headed back into the common room. Obviously, she didn't see this woman as a threat to her territory.

"May I come in?" she asked. Her voice was deep and musical.

My mother said nothing, only held the door open for her to enter. She was soaked through, the water dripping from her cloak creating little puddles on the ground.

Leaf, our visitor is a woman. I sent. *I think she might be one of mother's friends from the Royal Army.* I couldn't think of who else it would be, otherwise. There was something about her, though, something about her face that was familiar to me, as if I had seen it in a painting or a book before.

"You shouldn't be here," said my mother.

At first I thought she was talking about me, but she was looking at the visitor, all of her attention focused on her guest. Was this the "she" that Uncle Lenatus had spoken of? I could still hear their argument from that night in our suite.

The woman smiled wryly as she hung her cloak on a

hook. She wore the same uniform mother often did, the dark red jacket and black breeches of an Officer of the Royal Army. "You would not have come to me at the Palace even if I had ordered you to, Augusta." She smiled, showing pearly white teeth. "Always the stubborn one, even after all these years."

"You know I couldn't even if I had wanted to, Sofiya," my mother shot back. "You shouldn't be here, what if someone saw you?"

Sofiya's grin widened. "They didn't see me," she said. "Anyone looking would have seen an Officer in the Royal army. She raised a hand and rested it against my mother's cheek. "You worry too much, my Augusta."

"I have much to worry about," said my mother.

The other woman smiled. "No, you just think you do," and then she kissed my mother.

It was not simply a peck on the cheek, it was a mouth kiss, the like of which I had never seen before. I quickly turned away, suddenly filled with the sense that I should not be watching the two participate in such an intimate activity.

Hedda? What's wrong? Leaf asked, sounding anxious. *Why are you embarrassed?*

My mother is kissing the visitor. I replied.

Oh, I could feel Leaf's embarrassment through the bond.

Are you going to go up to our room, then?

It seemed like the sensible thing to do, but something was still bothering me about our visitor. She seemed so familiar, where had I seen her before---

--The Queen!

I felt a pang of fear from an obviously started Leaf. *Hedda!* She cried. *You startled me! I---did you say the Queen?!*

Of course! Why hadn't I seen it sooner! Her face was stamped on all of our coins, after all, and her name, Sofiya, there was only one Sofiya that I knew of that lived in the Palace, or who would be important enough as to be forced to sneak out of the Palace disguised as a member of the Royal Army.

My mother is kissing Queen Sofiya.

It was impossible, and yet, the evidence was right before my eyes. It still didn't explain many things, but suddenly I thought I understood why my mother had been acting so strange since we had arrived in Firehaven.

My mother had wrapped her arms around the Queen as they kissed, but now she withdrew, breathless. "Holy Powers," she breathed. "I missed doing that…."

The Queen smiled up at her. "You have no idea how much I missed you, Augusta, what I had to do while you were away—No, no, let's not think on that." She tilted her head up to kiss my mother on the mouth again, but briefly this time. "Come to bed with me tonight, Augusta. You have been gone far too long."

My mother grinned, kissing the top of her head. "I thought I was supposed to be the one issuing the invitation, Sofiya," she teased.

Queen Sofiya chuckled. "A woman in my position is used to making invitations."

"I thought you had servants for that sort of thing," mother teased, still grinning. She wrapped her arms around the Queen again and drew her close. "We won't have time to do much…." She warned. "I do have a daughter and two spirits to care for."

Sofiya nodded. "I will wait here," she said. "Are you sure you don't want me to—"

My mother paused mid-step. "I don't want her brought into his games," she said firmly. "Does he still have an invitation to your bed, or have you finally kicked him out for good this time?"

Sofiya sighed. "His invitation has not been officially revoked, but I have not....been with him....since Luccia was born. I have kept him busy building bridges and towers when he isn't campaigning." She smiled sadly. "He seems to think that if he can impress me with the most outlandish designs, I will decide that I do not loathe him."

I suddenly realized that if I remained in this spot any longer, one or both of them would notice me, and so, carefully so as not to make any noise, I left my hiding spot and headed to the common room.

As soon as I slipped into the common room I was accosted by an excited Leaf.

"I heard everything that you did!" She exclaimed. "It seems like we finally found an answer, Hedda!"

"Yes," I agreed. "But that's just one answer; we still have many questions to answer, yet."

"Well, have they moved away from the front door, yet?" Leaf asked. "We could follow th—"

I blushed. "No, no! I don't think we need to follow them just now!" I said hastily.

"Why?" Leaf asked, a curious expression on her face. Near the hearth fire, Ember started to laugh as my face grew red. "Leaf, do you remember the Temple of Ilisith, and what Savant Chesnos told us?" I asked.

Leaf's expression turned thoughtful, and then realization dawned on her face. "Oh, yes, I sometimes forget that humans have a complicated mating process."
Ember was laughing so hard she fell into the fire. Leaf glared at her. I could not seem to stop blushing.

"I think that it would be wise to sleep in one of the

downstairs bedrooms tonight," I remarked.

The next morning, the Queen's cloak was gone from the hook, and mother seemed to be in unusually high spirits. When I asked her about the visitor who came last night, she replied that they had spent the night getting reacquainted.

Reacquainted, indeed! Leaf chortled, and I nearly choked on my food.

Leaf! I'm trying to eat!

I'm sorry, Hedda! She replied, but she didn't sound very apologetic to me.

I spent the morning with Uncle Lenatus, learning more about how to draw on Leaf's power to accomplish feats that I normally would not be able to do on my own.

"Eldermaids are highly sought by nobles because of their ability to grant their bondmate immunity to poisons," he explained. "Their bondmates make excellent food tasters, but even more efficient assassins. It's a mixed blessing, bonding to an eldermaid."

"I don't understand why everyone seems to think you must be one thing because you bonded to a certain spirit!" I complained. "I don't want to be an assassin or a food taster; I just want to be me!"

Uncle Lenatus nodded. "I understand, child, but most simply see it as a role that spirit plays best, and can't seem to imagine their bonded being anything else. It is as difficult to put a knight on the front lines as it is to put a maid in charge of strengthening a wall. My advice to you is to make yourself into the kind of woman you want to be, but to keep Leaf's strengths in mind." He grinned suddenly. "I would definitely not recommend the life of a sailor, though, on those rickety wooden boats all the time. A ship is no place for a treemaid, in my opinion."

In the afternoon, I received some instruction in the use of my glaive and dagger from mother.

"Remember, Hedda," she said. "The glaive can be used as both a slashing and stabbing weapon, but take care that the pole doesn't take too much abuse."

"I don't understand why you need to learn about fighting and killing," Leaf remarked from where she watched off to the side, folding her arms across her chest.

"It could save her life one day, Leaf," mother replied. "Every soldier learns these techniques in the hope that they will never have to use them, but they know them, just in case…." She slashed at the wooden dummy's side.

"Just in case," she repeated. "Besides, I'll sleep better knowing my Hedda can take care of herself when I'm not around."

Leaf frowned but she offered no further comment. Mother kept me at it until the sun was beginning to sink just below the horizon. By the time I went to bed that evening, I was exhausted and ready for sleep, and I envied Leaf for the boundless energy that she seemed to have.

I quickly settled into this routine: lessons with Uncle Lenatus and the acolytes in the morning, training with my mother in the afternoon. Every so often, mother would break up this routine with a trip to the market or the theatre. It was during one of those trips--when we had been in the city for two years--that another piece of the puzzle fell into place.

CHAPTER EIGHT

It was the beginning of autumn, when summer's heat made way for winter's chill, when mother decided to take a trip to the market while fresh produce was still available. It was the perfect day for such a trip. The trees were just turning shades of red and orange and the air was crisp but it was not especially chilly. Leaf, too, was not immune to the changes. She had traded summer's green for yellow. She was not the only one, of course, I saw many tree spirits out and about with their bondmates, all turning various shades: red, orange, even dark purple.

Mother was occupied filling a basket of fresh vegetables, so I took Leaf to the part of the market where they were selling breads and preserves. There was a merchant there, Galahan

Kaddles, who always took Leaf's elderberries in exchange for a loaf of bread and a jar of apple jelly.

"There's no finer elderberry jam than the jam that's made with an elder spirit's berries," he'd say, and I would be reminded of Igraine, who said the exact same thing. This time, though, I had to scramble to pluck all the berries before they fell to the ground. On this particular trip, I didn't find very many berries, but Mr. Kaddles just smiled and gave me the bread and jelly anyways.

"I'm always grateful for whatever you can give, Ms. Hedda," he said. "The berries alone will fetch a good price at market."

I thanked him and went off in search of mother, Leaf following close behind me, when I nearly ran into a young boy. He was dressed plainly in shades of brown and green with dark hair, slightly pink skin, and crystalline blue eyes.

"Xe wants to see you," he said to me.

I stopped midstride, not expecting to be approached in any way. "Who wants to see me?" I asked, completely and utterly confused.

That is probably the oddest thing I have ever heard anyone say, Leaf remarked, and I had to suppress the urge to chuckle.

The expression on the boy's face said that I ought to know who was asking for me, but he tersely replied. "The Rogue of Firehaven, of course," in a way that suggested I should be familiar with the name.

"I didn't know Firehaven had a Rogue," I replied. Urban areas had their own spirits--metal spirits in particular were more common in cities--but for a Rogue to bond to an entire city? I had never heard of such a thing. Although, given the capricious nature of jacks, a Rogue bonding with a city was not an impossibility, but a city as large as Firehaven? That would be quite the feat indeed.

The boy sighed; clearly, this was not going the way he'd hoped. "Xe wants to see you," he repeated, grabbing hold of my sleeve. "Come on!"

"No!" I cried, pulling away from him. "I'm not going anywhere with you!" I was certain this was a ploy to lure me into an alley, but even if it wasn't I wasn't just going to go with him because he said that someone—even if xe was a spirit—wanted to see me.

Leaf moved to plant herself between us, and I took the opportunity to put as much distance from the boy as I could, weaving in and out of the crowd. I nearly crashed into someone who was standing at a fishmonger's stall, only managing to avoid him at the very last second thanks to reflexes honed by mother's training.

Leaf caught up to me behind a stand that was selling oil cakes. "He ran away when you did, in the opposite direction," she said.

"Let's just find mother," I said, scanning the area for any sign of her or Ember. "Can you call to Ember?"
Leaf closed her eyes for a moment. "This way," she said. "They are wondering where we went off to."

Mother didn't ask either of us many questions about where we had been, but she was delighted with the jelly and bread. Truth be told, I didn't know what to tell her. I revisited the incident over and over in my mind. It made about as much sense now as it did then, that is, none at all.

"Mother," if there was a bonded spirit in Firehaven, surely she would know of them. "Have you ever heard of a spirit called the Rogue of Firehaven?" I asked.

Mother frowned. "I can't say I have, Hedda. Where did you hear about this spirit?"

"When we were exploring the market, I heard someone mention a Rogue of Firehaven," I explained. "I thought you might know something about it."

"I should think it would be difficult for a spirit to bond to an entire city," Ember mused. "Even jacks have their limits, though they often do not believe it is so."

Mother nodded in agreement. "Indeed, if there is a spirit claiming to have—or, Powers forbid, has—bonded with the city, xe must be a very powerful spirit indeed. I certainly wouldn't want to cross a spirit that powerful."

On the walk home, I tried to put the boy from the market out of my mind. The scent of the fresh bread mother had bought helped somewhat, as did helping our cook—a thin retired soldier by the name of Sir Palverel –with preparing the meal. It was hard to think on such things when you were so focused on chopping vegetables.

Surprisingly, mother never said a word about the market, instead praising Leaf and I on the progress we had made in our lessons.

"Your uncle is especially pleased with how quickly Leaf has been able to create and use poison darts," she remarked, taking another sip of her soup. "It's a useful skill in a fight, Hedda. A skilled treemaid can drop a skilled soldier without laying a hand on them—not that I want you killing on the streets, of course," she added, gesturing to me with her spoon. "And you, Hedda, have been making good progress with your glaive. Soon, you might even be able to take on Sebastian."

I glanced over at our butler, who smiled shyly at me.

"Sebastian knows how to wield a glaive?"

"Of course he does," she replied matter of factly. "All of the servants know somewhat of self defense, who else is going to defend my home if it was ever attacked while I was away?"

My eyes widened. "You taught….all of the servants?"

Mother shook her head. "Not all of them, obviously, the ones who have served us for generations—Sebastian's family, for instance—have been training their children for years, but I've made sure that everyone at least knows how to wield a good cast iron frying pan. It's traditional for Officers in the Royal Army to have household staff who are more….knowledgeable….in the Way of War than most."

"Oh," was all I could manage in response. I glanced at Leaf, who shrugged and went back to drinking her water. All of a sudden, Ember perked up. "Someone is knocking on the door," she said.

Sebastian glanced at Ember; then slipped out of the room. He was back in minutes, carrying what looked like a letter in his hand. "A letter for you, Hedda," he said, presenting it to me.

The letter was sealed with a wax seal as red as dried blood. There was nothing written on it to indicate where it was from, although "Lady Hedda" was written on the reverse in elegant cursive. I did not recognize the seal.

Leaf and Ember were both looking over my shoulder, now. "Open it, Hedda," Leaf breathed.

I broke the wax seal and unfolded the letter. It was written in the same elegant script as my name on the reverse, and read:

Dear Lady Hedda,

I was most aggrieved that you did not accept my man's invitation to meet with me this afternoon at the market. I assume that this is because he was rather uncouth in his manner of speaking. For that, I sincerely apologize, I had instructed him to be polite when speaking to you. I do not blame you for running from him.

I do, however, cordially invite you to meet with me at your earliest convenience. Simply head to the Temple of Menaishe in the Old City and one of mine will collect you. You may bring Leaf with you, of course, but no others, and rest assured, I will know if you do, just as I know that Ember is reading over your shoulder as you read this. She cannot see this message.

I would very much appreciate your cooperation in this matter. Your mother is going to arrange for you to spend the day at the Temple of Sudrask, I suggest you take the time during lunch to meet with me. Do not worry about not being back on time, everything has already been arranged for your visit.

The Rogue of Firehaven

"Well, that's strange," Ember remarked as I pocketed the letter. "I wasn't aware that you had an admirer, Hedda! Did you meet her at the Temple of Ilisith?"

I felt my cheeks redden. *Of all the things the Rogue of Firehaven could have said in xir letter!* I exclaimed to Leaf.

Play along, Hedda, came the reply, but I could have sworn she was trying hard not to laugh.

To my credit, I guess I looked embarrassed enough that Ember didn't question me when I said "I might have met someone…."

Mother grinned. "I remember my first love," she said wistfully. "Ember burst in on us and almost fried her to a crisp!"

"How was I supposed to know that you weren't moaning

because you were in pain?!" Ember snapped.

Mother burst out laughing. I felt my cheeks redden even more. It was one thing, my having a lover; it was a whole other thing to imagine my mother having one—even after what I'd witnessed with the Queen.

"May I be excused?" I asked, eager to pore over the contents of the letter in private with Leaf.

My mother made a dismissive gesture. "Go ahead, Hedda," but as I turned to leave, she said. "You know love is nothing to be ashamed about, right sweetheart?"

"I know, mother," I replied. "It's just…."

Mother nodded sagely. "I understand, I was once your age myself."

I nodded, and then, Leaf in tow, I left the dining room.

"I can't believe anyone would write such a thing!" I fumed as I paced in our room, Leaf watching worriedly from her pan of water. "Me!? With anyone!? That's the silliest thing I've ever heard!"

Leaf shrugged. "How did the Rogue of Firehaven manage to make it so that Ember read something different than what we read?"

I paused mid-stride, considering her question.

"I guess it was some sort of illusion," I mused. "I've heard jacks are very good at creating illusions. Mother says that's why they're so valuable to the Royal Army, because a skillful illusion can cause enemy soldiers to panic. Jacks don't bond easily though, so there aren't very many of them currently serving in the army."

Leaf looked thoughtful. Even though we had been together for a while now, it was still odd seeing an expression that was so human on her face.

"What are we going to do, Hedda?" She asked finally.

I didn't want to do it, but this Rogue of Firehaven didn't seem like xe was the type of spirit who would take no for an answer. The subtle threat underlying the polite wording was obvious. If only I could show the letter to Ember or mother, then—

No, what could they possibly do to help, except perhaps to go themselves, and the fact of the matter was, even if I had wanted to show them the letter, I could not.

In the end, I didn't have much choice.

I went to the chest at the foot of my bed and took my glaive and dagger, sliding the former in place against my back and the latter in its sheath at my side. "I guess we have no choice, Leaf," I said. "Come on; let's go meet this Rogue of Firehaven...."

Leaf gave me a thoughtful look, and then she held up a hand. "Wait, Hedda," she said. "Perhaps we could ask Flower about the letter? Even if xe can't break the illusion on it, maybe xe can tell us something about the sender."

Well, I wasn't sure that Ser Flower would be able or willing to tell us anything, but it was certainly better than walking headlong into a potentially dangerous situation.

"Okay," I said. "Let's hope xe can help us."

"Let me see if I understand you correctly," said Flower as xe took the letter from me. "You wish for me to ascertain whether this letter is covered by an illusion spell?"

"Yes, Ser Flower," I said. "We would really appreciate it if you would—"

"--No," said Flower.

I confess I was a little taken aback by the terseness in xir voice. "No?"

"No, there is no illusion on this letter," Flower clarified, waving the letter a little to emphasize xir point. "Or, at least, none that I can detect, and there are very few illusions that a jack can create through which another jack cannot see." Xe handed the letter back to me. "Therefore, either this Rogue of Firehaven you speak of is exceptionally powerful, which, being a Rogue, xe is likely to be, or you and your Leaf are delusional."

I scowled. "Neither of us are delusional," I stated. Flower shrugged slightly. "Well then, far be it for me to suggest that you should have any dealings with this Rogue—if, indeed, you are not merely playing a prank on me with this insipid love confession. All the land-bonded spirits can be dangerous, but Rogues are dangerous in their unpredictability…."

"I thought you said that not all jacks are chaotic," I said, unable to hide my smile.

Flower glared at me. "No, we are not all such temperamental beings, but it would behoove you to be cautious, all the same." Xe waved a hand at me in dismissal. "Now, run along, I have a temple to oversee, and do not have time to entertain your flights of fancy."

"Well, that wasn't very helpful," I complained to Leaf as we walked along the road towards the city gates. "What do we do now, Leaf?"

Leaf sighed. "I guess we have no choice," she said. "Who knows how the Rogue will react if we keep refusing to meet with xir?"

I shook my head. "I don't know, and I don't want to find out, but…." I took Leaf's hand. "If we're going to go, we need to be very, very careful…."

"I know," Leaf replied, squeezing my hand. "I'll be careful if you'll be careful, Hedda."

"   Always," I promised.

"Good," Leaf said, nodding to herself. "If we're going to meet xir, we should go before the sun sinks below the horizon, there's no telling who—or what—we'll encounter after dark."

Firehaven's Old City was once the seat of government before Queen Lesith the Great moved the capital further south, but the old Temple of Menaishe was still in use. It was an imposing structure, with giant braziers of flame constantly burning brightly near the front of the building. A great many blacksmiths worked under the shadow of the temple dedicated to their divine patroness. It took some coaxing to convince Leaf to even approach the temple at first, for she was understandably nervous due to all the fires in the area, but eventually she appeared to muster her courage and walked with me along the cobblestone path between the temple, a few smithies, and a tavern known as the Golden Flame.

We did not get far before a woman approached us. She had long hair that was as white as snow, skin as dark as Uncle Lenatus', and sized us up with steel grey eyes. She was dressed in black from head to toe, with a couple of daggers and a sword buckled at her side. Following close behind her was another woman

No, I realized as we came closer, not a woman, but a seamaid.

It is difficult to tell spirits apart from people at times. It might seem like an odd thing to say, but for one who has not regularly encountered spirits, they could easily be mistaken for humans in costume, but sea spirits tended to have less obvious otherworldly markers than their kin of tree and flame. This one's true nature was exposed by her bright blue hair and eyes, as well as the fact that she had gill slits. Many tales have been told of less observant humans who had attempted to ravish seamaids, to their peril.

"Good, you're here," was all the woman said, gesturing for us to follow her. I quickly fell into step behind the seamaid, Leaf following behind me. I wanted to ask where we were going, but truth be told, I didn't think the woman looked like the type of person who would tolerate such questions.

"I haven't the slightest idea why xe wants to see you," the woman remarked suddenly. "You're just a child, aren't you?"

"I had my first moonblood a couple years ago," I replied.

"Still a child, then," she said, and I bristled a little at the dismissive tone in her voice. "I still have no idea why xe wants to meet with you…."

The rest of our walk was spent in silence except for the sound of her boots striking the cobblestones. Once or twice, I glanced around to see if I could recognize any of the buildings, any landmark that might lead me back to where I started, but the buildings in this section seemed to blend together. I couldn't tell where one ended and another began. It was as if we were wandering through a dreamscape than the Old City, it was disconcerting, to say the least. A few of the buildings we passed had small windows. I thought I saw one or two with a small effigy of Kamalak, God of Thieves, surrounded by dried flowers and offerings of food and drink—likely ale. Even though he was called God of Thieves, many also prayed to Him for justice if they were the victims of a theft, and He was also known as the Luckgiver, the Patron of Gamblers, and was said to be fickle with His favours.

At last, the woman paused at a door that, as far as I could tell, was identical to many of the doors we had passed already.

How she knew which one to open, I hadn't the slightest idea. She gestured for Leaf and I to enter first. As much as I didn't want this strange woman at my back, there was little sense in arguing the point, so I simply took a deep breath and stepped over the threshold, Leaf following close behind me. A soon as we stepped inside I heard the door swing shut and the click as it was locked behind us.

Leaf? Do you think you can break down that door if we need to get out quickly? I asked.

I don't know, Leaf admitted. *If the Rogue of Firehaven really is bonded to the city, xe could easily make it so I would be unable to break through.*

And with that comforting thought, we headed deeper into the Rogue's domain.

The inside of the building put me in mind of a temple. It was softly lit and I could smell smoke from incense I could not identify, at least, I thought it was incense. The smoke was thick in the room. It felt like I was in a strange dreamscape.

I yelped suddenly as I ran into some sort of fabric that seemed to have materialized out of thin air. I managed to push it away, but behind me, I could hear the woman chuckle. I wasn't sure that she could see my glare in the haze, but I glared anyways. Leaf placed a comforting hand on my shoulder.

It's all right , she assured me. *It's just fabric hanging from the ceiling.*

I glanced up, and, sure enough, the diaphanous fabric did seem to be hanging from the ceiling, although the smoke was so thick I couldn't make out any other details. It reminded me of a shop from a faraway land. For all I knew, all of this was an elaborate illusion created by the Rogue of Firehaven to confuse people, perhaps to intimidate potential enemies, or, well, who knew why a Rogue did anything?

I spent what seemed like several minutes weaving around more of the hangings. They were almost like banners, except I could not see any design that indicated whose banners they were.

"How much longer 'til we get to speak to the Rogue?" I asked, head beginning to pound from all the smoke in the room.

"Just keep walking," came the terse reply.

I sighed and turned my attention to my feet. *One more step, two more steps, three more steps….* I chanted. *Four more steps, five more steps….*

Then, suddenly, the fog of incense cleared and I was standing in front of a door. It was made entirely out of metal, and had no handle that I could see, only a curious embossed brass design depicting a coiled serpent, its mouth partially open. The door also had a sizable gap in it, directly below the serpent, a narrow passageway connecting the two. If it was the door's handle, it was the strangest one I had ever seen, and I could see no way to open it from our side. As I watched, the woman reached into the serpent's mouth and pressed the pad of her finger against one of its fangs.

The serpent's eyes lit up with a bright golden glow.

I jumped back, startled. The serpent was moving as if it was a living thing, uncoiling and slithering through the narrow passageway and into the gap below, where it coiled up again.

"Sudrask!" I exclaimed, awed by the mechanical marvel before me, but the woman only gave me an impatient glare. "What happens if the wrong person puts their finger in there?" I asked.

"They lose it," she replied matter-of-factly, striding through the door, her seamaid following. "Come on, hurry up!" She snarled. "You don't want to be stuck on the other side alone!"

I hurried through the door, looking back over my shoulder to see if Leaf was behind me, sighing in relief when I saw that she had not left my side.

Then I turned my attention to what was in front of me, and I saw that we had arrived.

The massive room in which Leaf and I found ourselves seemed to be a mixture of throne room and magpie's hoard. Crates were stacked along one wall, and theatre masks shared space with empty bottles of wine. There were piles of coins and weapons, charms made with locks of human hair, horseshoes and rabbit feet hanging on lengths of cord, and other objects that I couldn't even name.

The people in the room were no less diverse than the objects that surrounded them. I didn't know what to expect from the Rogue of Firehaven's Court, other than brawny, unkempt men, like the sort I read of in storybooks who haunted taverns, drinking and fighting. As I glanced around, however; I saw people of all ages, colors, shapes, sizes, and sexes. Some were playing at dice, others seemed to be adding objects to the many piles in the room, most of them didn't even look up when my companion and her seamaid entered the room, much less pay any attention to the two figures trailing along behind them.

At least one did, however.

My attention was drawn towards xir like a moth to flame. Xe sat in a great metal throne, one leg carelessly thrown over the other. The boy from the market was near to xir, crouched down and concentrating on something: a game using small stones as game pieces. Flanking the Rogue on either side were two metalmaids, standing still and silent as statues. Metal spirits were a strange breed; metalknights were particularly valued for their nigh indestructibility, which made them ideal candidates to reinforce defensive walls and siege engines. It used to be that this was accomplished by incorporating the spirit themselves into the walls, but that was quickly condemned as unnecessarily cruel to both spirit and bondmate, and so nowadays this was accomplished by inserting a small piece of a spirit into the wall in the same way that spirits bonded to humans. Some grumbled that the walls were not as strong as when the spirit was directly encased into the metal, but most agreed that it was necessary to preserve the sanity of both spirit and their human partner.

The Rogue of Firehaven shifted in xir seat a little as the woman approached xir. It was then that I noticed something curious about xir, the fact that xir face was shrouded in shadow even though there was abundant light in the room. Oh, I could see that xe had black hair and brown skin that was a mixture of the many shades that humans possessed, but xir finer features were obscured from my sight. That was even more disconcerting to me than the fact that I could not tell what sort of spirit xe had been before xe became a Rogue. Most spirits, like Leaf, bore telltale signs of their heritage, but the Rogue of Firehaven was different. Xe appeared, for all intents and purposes, to be as human as I was, with none of the telltale signs that xe was something other than human.

I wondered if it was possible that xe was a new type of spirit, a young spirit. The Savantry of Sudrask was always eager to uncover new kinds of spirits, and I could not imagine one— even one as powerful as the Rogue of Firehaven—escaping their notice.

"I've brought you the girl, Boss," the woman was saying. "She's in one piece and only mildly shaken." I heard her smile, even though all I could see was her seamaid's backside.

The Rogue of Firehaven nodded slightly. "Indeed you have. Thank you, Avna, you may go and rest with Crest, if you wish," xe smiled, and xir smile was like a sharpened knife. "Or you may stay, I think you will find this discussion most....enlightening."

The way xe said "enlightening" made me think that xe had meant to say "entertaining" but that thought was quickly whisked away as xe turned xir attention to me.

It is difficult to describe, even now, how xir gaze affected me. It felt as if a giant weight had settled on my shoulders, and I suddenly felt the strong urge to turn away from xir, even though I could not see xir eyes. Impulsively, I reached out and touched Leaf's mind through the bond, and was met by a jumble of feelings: confusion, curiosity, and fear. The latter was particularly strong, and I had to break the connection between us before her fear started to affect me.

The Rogue of Firehaven smiled again, and this time, I tried to return xir smile.

"Sit," xe said, snapping xir fingers, and I nearly jumped out of my skin as a chair appeared out of thin air and I fell into it.

"We have much to discuss," xe continued, leaning back in xir throne and steepling xir fingers. "Where to begin, I wonder?"

I could not hold it in any longer.

"Why did you contact me?" I blurted out. "Ever since I moved to this city, it seems as if everyone has a secret to keep and no one is sharing at all, especially not with me!"

The Rogue of Firehaven shrugged slightly. "I asked for you because you are, at the moment, in the right position at the right time, like a well-placed Flamemaid in the Game of Spirits—generally useless in any other context, but when played in the right place at the right time, quite useful, indeed."

Xe smiled again, and this time I saw a flash of pearly white teeth.

"Or a Treemaid, if you prefer," xe continued. "I do think that is more appropriate, given your circumstances," xe indicated Leaf with a nod of xir head, and Leaf, to my surprise, actually flinched under the weight of xir gaze.

She's feeling as uneasy as I am right now. I thought. Who wouldn't be, given our situation?

The Rogue was waiting for a response. I considered the implications of xir words. "So what you are saying is that I'm a useful tool." I said tentatively.

The Rogue of Firehaven shrugged. "All humans are tools, to some degree, whether to each other, or to the spirits, or even to the Powers Themselves," xe gave me the knife-smile again. "You might as well become used to being a tool, Hedda. Others who will seek to use you will not be as forthcoming about it as I have been, I can promise you that."

"Forthcoming?" I scowled. "So far, you have not told me much of anything, and you expect me to cooperate because you are at least being honest about your motivations? Why? I'm no one special. My mother is an Officer in the Royal Army—"

"—Do you know," interjected the Rogue of Firehaven "—who your father is?"

I froze, of all the questions xe could have asked, xe had chosen this one. "No," I admitted. "Mother never talked about him, or much of her past in Firehaven."

"Ah, you see," the Rogue grinned. "That is where we may help each other."

"I didn't realize I had agreed to help you," I muttered, glancing around at the other people in the room, who were, for the most part, paying no attention to what was going on near the throne. "They're criminals, aren't they? I won't help criminals."

The Rogue shrugged. "They are merely victims of circumstance. Society brands them criminals because they do what must be done to survive." Xe shrugged. "Can you blame a person who is only trying to survive in this world?"

Before I could respond, xe smiled again, more confidently this time. "And I do not recall giving you a choice in the matter, my dear Hedda, the manipulator seldom gives the manipulated a choice, only various options that lead to the same goal."

Xir words sent a chill down my spine, but as long as there were questions with no answers, I needed to keep asking. "And what is your goal?" I asked. "Or am I not supposed to know that yet."

"Oh, my goal is a simple one," the Rogue replied. "The wellbeing of my people," and here xe made a grand gesture encompassing the whole room "is and will always be my goal."

"Then why not go to the Queen?" I asked. "Surely she would listen to a spirit as powerful as yourself?"

I could not see the Rogue's face, but I felt xir anger deep in my bones. "The Queen of Firehaven cares not for the plight of my people. She sets her General on them like a trained hound; then turns a blind eye while their blood runs in the alleys." Xe spat, and where the spittle landed, the carpet smoked.

"But—" I bit my lip, glancing around at the people in the room again. My mother had always taught me that criminals needed to be brought to justice, and that the law was fair, only truly punishing those guilty of horrific crimes "—is that not the way it is supposed to work?"

"Oh, indeed, I forget how naïve you are," said the Rogue.

"Let me see if I understand you. The way of the world is that the guards, who work to protect this fair city, bring criminals to justice, is that correct?"

I had a feeling I wouldn't like where this conversation would end, but I nodded.

"Ah, yes, a very clean way of viewing the world," the Rogue remarked. "Good triumphing over evil, right over wrong, yes, very neat." Xe leaned forward in xir chair, the shadows seeming to move with xir to obscure xir features. I wondered, was xe doing this to throw me off guard, or did xe have something to hide, a scar, or some telltale sign of the sort of spirit xe'd been before xe had become the Rogue of Firehaven. I couldn't think of any spirit that had the power to manipulate shadows the way xe was doing.

"Now, let me tell you how it really works," xe said. "In the Firehaven of today, the guards will run a child through for so much as stealing a loaf of bread to feed their hungry siblings. There is no justice except for the nobility, who live by exploiting those too poor to ever afford proper justice for themselves. In the past, they at least had a sporting chance at surviving their ordeal, but not now, not in the Firehaven of today. That is what I seek to change, and you are going to help me change it, Hedda."

Suddenly, it was as if the pieces of a great puzzle fell into place.

Change....

"Who are you?" I whispered.

The Rogue smiled again, and then xe leaned forward, the shadows that obscured xir features drawing aside like a curtain opening on a play, and I beheld xir face at last.

Dark, wavy black tresses framed a face with russet skin, a hawk-like nose, and high cheekbones, and then there were xir eyes, sweet Powers, those eyes….

I knew who xe—or rather, He--was the instant my eyes gazed into His. They were twin black pools, and the more I gazed at them, the more I felt as if I was going to be sucked into them. Moving within that inky darkness, I could see stars wink in and out, exploding and reforming, saw the bright tail of a comet as it streaked through the sky. I might have been lost in that gaze forever if He had not chosen to shut His eyes, and the universe behind them simply winked out of existence. I fell to my knees on the red carpet, not only out of respect and awe, but also because I was so overwhelmed by what I had seen.

It is said that the Powers left the world, but it is also said that some of Them remained behind.

"Well met, Hedda," said Kamalak, God of Thieves.

CHAPTER NINE

The tales that are told of Lord Kamalak are popular even with the children of the nobility, although nobles try to avoid speaking His name so as not to invite His notice. His sphere is Luck, and He is known to give Luck to His favourites, only to snatch it away when they become too greedy. He champions the oppressed and the downtrodden, the poor and the desperate. Many have argued that He was once a fifth aspect of Ilisith, others say that He is Ilisith's Son, born in the shadows. Thieves pray to Him to pass unseen in the night, while gamblers whisper His name before every throw of the dice. Until now, I had just assumed that the custom persisted because gamblers were known to be superstitious, but now I had to wonder if Someone was answering their prayers all along, and most simply did not want to consider that some people had never lost their Divine Patrons.

"Well met, Lord Kamalak," I mumured. "Why didn't You just tell me who You were in the first place?"

The god rose and came towards me, the shadows moving from the throne to cloak Him in darkness.

"Humans find it easier to believe in spirits than the Powers, these days," He remarked. "Tell Me, Hedda, would you have answered My call had that letter been signed 'Kamalak, God of Thieves', or would you have thrown it away, because everyone knows that all the Powers have left this world?"

I was going to tell Him that I had come close to throwing away the letter regardless of whose signature was attached to it, but instead I said. "I do not think I would have believed You."

"Indeed," said Kamalak. "Such is the way of the world, where few truly believe in any of Us, though some do still leave offerings and whisper prayers at My shrines."

"Do they—" I indicated the people milling around us. "Do they know—"

"That they unwittingly serve as savants to one of the Powers?" Kamalak supplied, grinning. "Most of them are content to believe—or are comfortable believing—that they simply serve a Rogue, though there are a few who know My true nature." He nodded to Avna and glanced down at the boy from the market, who continued to play his game, seemingly oblivious to what anything except his game. I had forgotten that Avna was still there, though I saw that she kept her eyes on me, even though I obviously posed no significant threat to her "Boss". No human could ever be a credible threat to one of the Powers. I supposed that this was a job which she was accustomed to performing, and the god did not seem to take offense to her presence in the least. He had offered to let her stay and observe us, after all.

I took a deep breath. "So, now that I know who You are, what is it You really want me to do?" I still didn't understand how I, a mere mortal, could possibly be of help to a deity, any deity.

"Get up off your knees, for starters," He replied, giving me a crooked grin. When I rose, he looked me over appraisingly, nodding to Himself.

"The second thing I want you to do is learn how to use that dagger of yours," he continued, indicating the weapon at my side.

"But, I do know how to use it. My mother taught me how to wield it!" I protested, glancing down at it as if His words had the power to dent the metal. Well, He was one of the Powers, surely He was capable of destroying a simple dagger if He chose to do so. .

All of a sudden, the dagger flew from my sheath and into the god's hand.

"Pah!" He spat. "You know how to flail about and hope that you might hit something!" He began idly tossing the dagger in the air and catching it "You need to actually learn how to use it, girl, and who better than a god to teach you? Thirdly—", and here the dagger flew from His hand and settled back into my sheath "—I suggest you ask your mother about your father."

"But couldn't you just tell me—"

Lord Kamalak wagged a finger at me, like a father scolding a child. "Do you expect me to live your life for you, girl?" He smiled, like a cat who had just caught a mouse. "No, no, that would hardly do, and it would ruin the surprise, and I quite like surprises, don't you?"

I scowled. "For someone who talks about needing me to help them, you aren't exactly being cooperative."

Hedda! Leaf cried. *He is a god, remember? Mind what you're saying!*

The god's eyes narrowed, the universe behind them narrowing

to mere pinpricks of stars.

"Do not mistake Me, girl," He murmured darkly. "There are such things I could steal from you. Your sanity, for one, or your life. It would be simple to steal the very breath from your lungs and use you as a puppet to achieve My ends. In that regard, you can consider My choice to leave you hale and whole to be a mercy, but a small one." And then the smile was back again, and it was like a stab to the heart. "Am I making myself clear?"

I thought my lip was going to burst from the way I was biting it, but I managed a nod. "Yes, Ser," I squeaked.

"Good," the air seemed to lighten as Kamalak walked back to His chair and settled into it. "See that you remember that when next we meet in the future, and every meeting after." When I nodded, He waved dismissively at us.

"Good, you may leave, for now." He said. "I expect to see you here again in two days, however."

"But how will I—"

Lord Kamalak gave me another cat-smile that reached all the way to His ears. "Do not worry about having to seek Me out, child--although, that would be an amusing game. No, a door shall appear when I have need of you, or I will send an escort. Either way, you shall have your lessons, and My people shall have their due, eventually."

As I turned to leave, He called to me. "Think on this girl, is it not ironic, that a Being as powerful as I should be forced to rely on mortals to accomplish My goals? My Father killed the Heretic King, but that was when He walked the land and His people knew Him, but now, none of Us can hope to match Him in strength, no matter how many still remember Me and leave Me offerings."

I was sure a savant could argue that that was not the case,

but I was no theologian.

The escort He sent with us to guide us back to the city was named Adebayo, who was much more talkative than brooding Avna, though his bondmate, who I was surprised to see was a metalmaid named Ore, was quiet. Men bonded to maids were especially sought after by the Royal Army, so I was curious as to why he was working for Kamalak instead of embarking on a successful career in the military.

Adebayo scoffed at this. "You might think it's glorious," he said. "But eventually I discovered that it wasn't the kind of life I wanted for myself, or my children. I was with them for two years, I have the scars to prove it, but....." He sighed. "They don't tell about all the bodies you have to climb over to get to all that fame and glory."

"And is working for the Rogue any easier?" I asked, thinking of all the people the God of Thieves had victimized through his Court.

"Well, I wouldn't say I work for Lord Ka—I mean, the Rogue," he corrected himself, winking at me. "Despite what you may think, many of us are good people, but even the best of people can come upon hard times. As a matter of fact, escorting you home is to be my last act in the Rogue's service, and from there, I go to the Temple of Ilisith. They've agreed to accept me as a savant provided I complete one of the Penances."

The Savantry of Ilisith preached that War was essentially polluting, for a warrior always kills someone's loved one, and so, to ensure that a person was truly dedicated to Love, the temple required all current and former members of the military to undergo a Penance, a task of some sort to atone for time spent under War's aegis. Penances were usually humiliating, though never sexual in nature. For more heinous crimes, such as rape and murder, the perpetrators were turned over the Savantry of Menaishe, who had a much more straightforward way of dealing with such criminals: imprisonment or death.

"I'm sure you'll do fine," I replied, smiling up at him.

"Well, I *have* managed to survive this long," he stated, returning my smile. "They even said they'd permit my husband to share my quarters at the temple."

Well, that was interesting. Savants of Ilisith didn't tend to enter long-term relationships, even after they had retired from temple life. "What does he think of your new….career path?" I asked.

Adebayo chuckled. "He's the one who suggested I study there, actually. We are both secure enough in our commitment to each other to be open to the occasional lover, and the temple does not always, if ever, require that kind of service of its savants, except by the mutual consent of all parties involved."

I thought that I would like to have a relationship as strong as the one that Adebayo had with his husband, but I had not given thought to matters of the heart since I had moved to the city. It seemed like such a small matter compared to what I was faced with now: a god giving me lessons in how to properly wield a dagger, finding out about my father, and Powers knew what else….

….and I had questions, still so many questions.

I was surprised to learn that not a lot of time had passed since Avna had come to escort me in the Old City and when Adebayo, Ore, Leaf, and I arrived at my house. When I said as much to Adebayo, he laughed.

"Yes, time flows differently in the Rogue's domain," he explained "to your delight or peril, depending on the circumstances of your meeting."

A chill went up my spine at the thought of what Kamalak would do to someone who had incurred His displeasure, but I hastily shoved it out of my mind before Leaf could pick up on it.

"Well, this is where we part ways," Adebayo continued. "For now, at least…." He gave me a final grin, raising a hand in salute before he turned and began walking in the direction of the Temple of Ilisith.

"Wait!" I called as he was leaving. "At least let me call for a carriage for you. It's a long walk to the temple."
Adebayo turned, giving me a wicked grin. "I already have a carriage of my own," he said, nodding to Ore.

As I watched, Ore seemed to melt, her body reshaping into a flat disk with a raised portion from which protruded two bars. I watched as Adebayo stepped onto the disk, grasping the bars—handles, I realized—tightly, all the while grinning hugely.

"They thought I was crazy, trying this with Ore," he said. "But there's no faster way to get around!" And, so saying, he sped away, laughing while Leaf and I just stood there, staring after him in shocked silence.

After a moment, I was able to speak.

"Leaf, do you think you and I could try something like that?"

Leaf quickly shook her head. "I think we should leave the load-bearing to the metal spirits," she said.

I heartily agreed with her.

CHAPTER TEN

"Mother, can you tell me about my father?" I asked that night after we had finished eating dinner. Thankfully, neither my mother nor any of the household staff had noticed our absence. I had Kamalak to thank for that. I wondered fleetingly if they sold small statuettes of Him in the marketplace, where I could purchase one. On second thought, I could imagine my mother's reaction if she found a statuette of the God of Thieves in our house, much less in my bedroom. My mother pursed her lips and Ember's expression changed to one of concern when she looked at her bondmate.

"You have no father, Hedda," Mother said at last. At the time, I didn't know how accurate that statement would turn out to be.

"But, mother!" I protested. "Doesn't everyone have a father? Is it so unusual that I'd want to know about mine?" Mother sighed. "What I meant, Hedda," she began, "is that there is a man who sired you, but he is not the same as a father who raises his children."

This was something I could understand. Many couples who were unable to have children visited the savants of Ilisith for just this reason, but mother had never said that I had been one of those children.

"Is my father a savant, then?" I asked. I could not see my mother taking a savant to bed, but until recently, I would not have believed that some of the Powers--apart from Yemena, of course--remained active in the world, and meeting with Kamalak had utterly shattered that belief.

My mother shook her head again. "No," she sighed. "He was a soldier, a very good soldier...."

Suddenly I thought back to the conversation mother had had with Queen Sofiya.

"I don't want her brought into his games,"

Who had she been talking about, then, my father?

"Mother, does this have something to do when you were last in the city?" I asked. I had almost said "with Queen Sofiya" but I recalled just in time that I was not supposed to have heard that conversation.

Mother sighed again. "Hedda, can this not wait until another time?" She stood, pushing her chair out. "I promise, I will answer all your questions eventually, but, not today. It has....been a rather trying day for me."

Later, I asked Sebastian what mother had been doing all day, for she had gone soon after I had arrived back at the house, and he replied with a vague explanation to the effect that mother had been entertaining a visitor at one of the local taverns.

I had a feeling that that visitor had been the Queen. No wonder my mother was exhausted.

I spent the rest of the evening with Leaf playing the

Game of Spirits. When we both grew bored of it, I put the cards away and we went into the yard to get a bit of practice in before the sun went down. I slashed and parried imaginary opponents with my glaive while Leaf, her arms elongated into spears, began her own killing dance. Uncle Lenatus had taught us that it was essential for tree spirits to keep moving in battle, as they were especially vulnerable to the enemy's flame spirits, so that is what we practiced: light, quick maneuvers designed to strike at an opponent suddenly and withdraw while they recovered.

"I still don't know how I feel about killing," Leaf admitted as we headed back inside. "Why else would everyone make us learn these things, if not to hurt or kill?"

"I know, Leaf," I said. "Let's just hope we never have to use half the stuff we've learned, okay?"

Leaf nodded. "We can only hope."

My training with Lord Kamalak began two days later. Igraine, Mother and Uncle Lenatus had taught me what they could of fighting honourably, but the techniques the god taught me took a decidedly darker turn.

"You will thank Me for this when you emerge still breathing from a battlefield." He remarked one day during a lecture about poisons. My other teachers had barely scratched the surface of this particular method of killing, as it turned out.

"The poison brewed from parts of an eldermaid is superior to anything brewed from a normal plant," Lord Kamalak explained. "Such a solution, when applied under the skin—say, on the point of a blade—can fell even the hardiest warrior as easily as a blade to the heart."

I knew this already, of course, but my practice sessions with Uncle Lenatus had never used actual poisons—nor ones so potent.

As promised, He also taught me some tricks with my dagger, like the fine art of throwing it in the air to distract someone while I skewered them through with my glaive, or the trick of reflecting light off its surface to blind my opponent.

"The niceties of polite, honourable warfare are for soldiers who do not care whether they live or die," He would explain as He went over the finer points of jamming a dagger into someone's eye. "But for those who care about survival, certain….liberties….need to be taken with the rules."

"The way thieves take liberties with their victims' belongings?" I asked.

The god gave me one of His knife-smiles. "There, now you are beginning to understand."

The last task He gave me to perform was to fight against a shadowy opponent He conjured up out of the air. "Make no mistake, girl," He said from His throne as I fought not to turn and flee from my opponent, who was at least twice my size and covered from head to toe in inky, black armor. "Her sword will hurt you if you give her an opening." He gave me another cat smile. "Be quick, and show no fear."

Are you ready for this, Leaf? I asked.

I'm ready. Leaf said. *Are you?*

Let's just hope Lord Kamalak doesn't let our opponent wound us too badly, I said, and then I drew my glaive and relaxed into the basic stance that my mother had taught me.

The shadow woman—I did not think it was a spirit—came at me so quickly that I barely had time to prepare for her strike. She had the obvious advantage of being taller than me, but my glaive was designed to make up for the disparity in our heights.

We danced. I tried to remember the steps that my various

teachers had taught me, but they fled in the face of the shadow's relentless assault. I did not think, I did not have time to think, only act. This wasn't like fighting against a practice dummy--who neither moved nor struck back in response to my assault--but something completely different. I cried out as the shadow woman landed a blow to my shoulder, so distracted by my own doubts that I forgot to watch where I was leaving openings that she could exploit.

Stupid, Hedda, stupid!

Leaf kept trying to circle around to her opponent's backside, but at the moment I was hit I heard her gasp in pain. The shadow woman simply turned and smacked her aside. Fortunately, I was able to recover quickly and use that moment of inattention to bring the flat of the glaive's blade down upon her head.

The shadow woman trembled and abruptly crumbled into dust. I winced as the pain in my shoulder flared up, but I managed to smile as I turned to regard Kamalak, still lounging on His throne.

"How did I do?"

In response, a searing pain seized me, and I fell to my knees.

"You were stupid," Kamalak snarled. "If your opponent had been wearing plate armor, that blow might have, at best, knocked them out for a few moments. Furthermore…." and here He glared at Leaf. "You were not making effective use of your skills, eldermaid, blunt force would have been much more effective against such an opponent. Only use darts when your opponent's flesh is exposed, and, if they are exposing a great deal of it, they do not deserve to win against you."

He rose from His seat, a sword suddenly appearing in His hand.

"Clearly, you need to learn what it's like to fight a proper opponent," He hissed, smiling in a way that said that I would not enjoy this lesson.

"Begin!" He commanded.

Kamalak spent what was probably several minutes but felt like close to an hour knocking me on my behind repeatedly. This time, Leaf and I worked in tandem, but our blows were like raindrops to Him, and the blows He gave us in return had all the force of a gale. By the time it was over, Leaf and I were exhausted and so bruised that I was sure my skin had turned a permanent shade of red and Leaf was bleeding sap all over the God of Thieves' floor.

"The lesson is finished for today," Kamalak murmured coldly, His sword disappearing as He went to sit on His throne again. "Avna will escort you out this time."

By the time we arrived back at the house, the pain and the bruises had faded, but the memory of how I had received them remained fresh in my mind, and, I could only assume, Leaf's mind as well.

Once again, no one appeared to notice that we had been gone. I suggested we head down to the kitchens to see if Ser Palverel had baked any bread this morning, but Leaf declined, stating that the fires made her nervous. I didn't blame her for this sudden outbreak of nerves, not after what Lord Kamalak had put us through.

"I'll be right back, then," I promised, parting ways with Leaf and heading down into the kitchens.

It was always hot in the kitchens due to the flame spirits that resided in the cooking fires, but none of the staff ever seemed to mind the heat. I was in luck, this day, for Ser Palverel had made fresh rolls with currants.

I had taken two rolls and was just about to spirit them

away to eat when I heard Leaf's frantic call.

Hedda! Come quick! She cried. *The Queen and a bunch of other people just stormed in and they're all headed up to Augusta's study. I think one of them is the Grandmistress of the Order of Menaishe.*

I froze, suddenly completely focused on receiving Leaf's message.

The Grandmistress of the Order of Menaishe is here? Are you sure? The head of the Order of Menaishe commanded the military in the monarch's name, and sometimes even served as Regent if the current monarch died without an heir, or with an heir who was too young to take the throne.

I can't be sure, Leaf replied. *But they all look pretty important. Should I follow them?*

Even though I knew it was wrong to eavesdrop, I was curious as to what so many important people were doing in my mother's study. I couldn't just sit there eating rolls with currants while I knew that something strange was happening in Firehaven. Lord Kamalak had said as much, and then there was the way mother had been acting ever since we had left the house with the elder tree behind.

I caught up to Leaf at the door to mother's study. *You didn't see any guards on the way up?* I asked.

Leaf shook her head. *No—well I did, but they weren't paying any attention to one little treemaid.*

Have they said anything important, yet? I asked.

Leaf shook her head. *Mostly the state of the realm, I think. They're having trouble with pirates around Seacliff, apparently.*

That doesn't surprise me, I replied. *Seacliff is a coastal city, after all.*

"Where is she, Augusta?" Someone—a woman—was saying. Was this the Grandmistress of the Order of Menaishe speaking, or someone else?

"Which 'she' would this be, Grandmistress?" My mother replied smoothly.

I heard the sound of a fist slamming against something hard—mother's desk, probably.

"You know who," the woman snarled. "Your daughter, you took a risk in bringing her here, Augusta."

"What was I supposed to do?" My mother snapped. "Did you really expect me to keep her isolated for the rest of her life, Yehmina? I'm not afraid of him."

"You of all people should know what he's capable of," Grandmistress Yehmina snapped. "We need to keep her safe, if Princess Luccia—"

"--Nothing is going to happen to my daughter," the Queen interjected, clearly annoyed by the implication in the Grandmistress' words.

"Apologies, Majesty," said Yehmina. "We won't allow anything to happen to your daughter—either of your daughters—if any of us can help it. But, none of this would have happened if Augusta hadn't returned to the city, mark my words."

"Let's just focus on the matter at hand," a male voice, this time. "Have your spies uncovered anything, Ser Kainet?"

I froze. *Kainet! The man from the tavern! Do you remember him, Leaf?*

Of course I do, Leaf replied. *The man with the treeknight, Seed, he works for the Queen?*

Apparently so, I replied. Had he been watching us before that night at the inn? Was that why mother had been less than pleased to see him that evening?

I turned my attention back to the meeting, Kainet was speaking now.

"—know about the planned attempt on Your Majesty's

life, of course, and we have safeguards in place" Kainet was saying. "As for anything else he may be planning, though, there are whispers, but I need a few days to verify the reports."

"We might not have a few days," Yehmina remarked bitterly. "You know what's at stake, Ser Kainet."

"I know," Kainet replied. "As m'lady Grandmistress keeps reminding me…"

I thought I heard someone—the Queen, most likely, giggle a bit, but all Yehmina said was "Knock it off, *Ser* Kainet."

"Well, then," the Queen was speaking this time. "If there are no other concerns, this meeting is hereby adjourned. You all have your duties."

"Yes, Your Majesty," came a chorus of voices.

Something about what the Grandmistress had said during the meeting bothered me, but I had to hastily duck out of the way as people started coming out of the study.

The first person to exit the room was the Grandmistress, at least, I assumed as much from the red armor she wore. Officers of the Order of Menaishe wore red on formal occasions, this I knew from my mother. Her hair was dark and cropped close to her head and her eyes were teardrop shaped. She paused to scan the hallway with narrowed eyes before stepping out of the room. I had the feeling that little escaped her notice. One did not get to be Grandmistress by being inattentive to their surroundings.

I held my breath as she glanced in the direction of my hiding place, only letting it out when she looked away.

I pressed my back against the wall and sighed in relief. When I poked my head out to look again, the hallway was empty. When I turned to speak to Leaf, however; I found there was a sword point hovering inches away from my throat.

"Thought you could hide, eh?" Grandmistress Yehmina smiled, showing her teeth. "A good try, girl, but you make more noise than a full regiment."

I was about to reply but mother poked her head out of the room, glancing at me, Leaf, and the Grandmistress in turn. "What's going on? Oh, for Menaishe's sake, Yehmina! Lower your sword, she's no threat to you."

"I caught this one loitering outside the room," Yehmina replied, slowly lowering her sword. "I thought your servants were trained not to eavesdrop, Augusta."

"She's not a servant." My mother beckoned for me, and when I came to her she slipped her arm around my waist. "This is Hedda….my daughter…."

The Grandmistress raised an eyebrow. "This is….?" Mother nodded. "She is."

Yehmina's expression softened into something unreadable, then, she gave me the barest hint of a smile. "Well met," she said, inclining her head slightly and sheathing her sword.

"Well met, ah, m'lady," I said, unsure of how to address the Grandmistress.

"Yehmina, what's going on? Who's there?" This time, it was the Queen who was speaking.

The Grandmistress turned to address her. "Just the daughter Augusta's been hiding from everyone, Your Majesty."

My mother scowled. "I haven't been hiding her!" She protested. "I just—"

And then the Queen appeared in the hall, and it was as if time had stopped in its tracks.

She wore a loose-fitting blouse with riding leathers, clothes that I would not have expected a monarch to wear, but then, this was the same Queen who had snuck out of the

Palace wearing an Officer's uniform. Her long tresses were tied back into a sensible bun. She wore few jewels, earrings, a necklace, and two rings on her fingers, and, of course, there was the sword hanging at her side. There was little doubt in my mind that it wasn't simply ornamental. Actually, there was little that would distinguish her from any other noblewoman, apart from her presence. She seemed to command my attention simply by being in the hall.

"Hello there, Hedda," she said softly, and I could have sworn I heard her voice crack as she said my name.

What do we do, Hedda? Leaf asked. *She's never been this close to us before.*

Well, what do you do when you meet one of your land-bonded sisters?

Oh, well, we just say hello.

I knew that I was probably supposed to curtsey, but I admit my education in courtly manners was sadly lacking. Mother had never been so strict about such things. "It's just you and me, Hedda," she would say with a smile. "There's no one out here to curtsey to…."

Even so, I managed to bob a little in imitation of others I had seen performing the gesture.

"Hello, er, Your Majesty," I said, blushing hotly at my own awkwardness.

The Queen smiled. "There now, no need to be so formal. Now, come here. Let me have a look at you…."

I stepped forward and the Queen gingerly reached out to grasp my chin and tilt my head upwards, looking at me with an expression of pure wonderment, as if she couldn't quite believe what she was seeing with her own eyes.

"She has his hair," she remarked to my mother.

"Indeed," my mother replied, smirking a little. "But she

has your nose...."

The Queen laughed. "Indeed, I should be grateful that she doesn't have his nose!"

But she has your nose.

We won't allow anything to happen to your daughter—either of your daughters....

It was like a dream, the kind of conversation I would have during my wildest childhood fantasies where I was a princess who lived in a castle with many toys and games to play, and soft kid gloves and ermine capes and the most delicate shoes.

"Mother, what is she talking about?" I asked, glancing over at the woman I'd always called mother, who had her arms folded across her chest.

Mother sighed. "I knew this day would come eventually, but...." She glanced at the Queen, who nodded, and then back at me.

"Hedda, the Queen, she's....she's your mother."

CHAPTER ELEVEN

The Queen is my—I stared at the woman she claimed was my mother. The Queen only smiled sadly.

"It's true, Hedda." She said. "I still remember the night you came into the world, such a long night, but all the pain was worth it." She brushed a stray hair out of my eyes.

"Ah, look at how you've grown!" She exclaimed. "Augusta must be feeding you the same things they feed the plants at the Temple of Kinarshe!"

I knew she spoke the truth, felt it deep in my bones.

All of a sudden, anger flared up inside me, and I turned to the woman I had thought was my only mother all these years. "When were you planning on telling me?!" I cried. "Why didn't you say anything?!"

It was the Queen who responded, though. "Hedda…." she began, glancing at my mother, as if for permission.

Mother gave the barest nod of her head, and then the other woman continued.

"Hedda," she said again. "Your mother couldn't tell you. She had a very good reason not to tell you. You were—we were all---we still are—in danger." She pulled me into an embrace before I could react. "I can't imagine how you must feel right now, my dear."

"I wish she would not have kept this from me," I muttered.

The Queen—my mother, one of my mothers—sighed. "I know, daughter. I know...." She released me from the embrace, holding me at arm's length. "You have a little sister who will be so pleased to meet you!"

"Princess Luccia?" I asked.

She nodded. "The very same." She glanced at my mother. "Maybe now we'll have a chance, Augusta."

My mother said nothing, her expression grave.

All of a sudden, there was a commotion from downstairs, and Sebastian came running.

"Majesty!" He cried, barely remembering to make any sort of obeisance. "He's here! He demanded to be let in to see you—I—I couldn't stop him!"

"Shhh, it's fine, Sebastian," my mother reassured him, laying a comforting hand on the anxious butler's shoulder. "Tell the staff to be ready."

Sebastian nodded. "Of course, m'lady. I'll send all the available bonded upstairs, just in case."

Mother and the Queen—it didn't seem right, calling her "mother" when we had only just met, although she had known me my whole life—both nodded, and then they turned as one to meet this mysterious "he" that everyone kept referring to in hushed tones with fear in their eyes.

"Quick, Hedda! You need to hide!" Mother hissed, already herding Leaf and I back behind the corner.

"Stay here," she ordered. "I mean it."

Together, the Queen and my mother turned to face the interloper.

The man who was climbing the stairs to meet them had red hair as bright as a bonfire at midnight. I could tell he was bulky even without his armor, which had the image of a golden lion on the breastplate. A flamemaid followed on his heels, a stony expression on her face. They were followed by an obviously irate Grandmistress of the Order of Menaishe.

"General, I thought I told you, the Queen is in council—" Yehmina was saying.

"—And as I told you, Grandmistress, I am a member of that same council, I have a right to be here," he replied smoothly as he climbed the stairs. When he reached the top, he gave my mother and the Queen an appraising look. Mother regarded him coolly, while the Queen's expression was carefully neutral.

There was a period of silence in which no one dared speak or move, and then the man smiled.

"Hello Augusta," he said.

"Hello, Lucian," she replied, with none of her usual warmth.

"I had thought you were out of the city on....extended leave...." said Lucian, his face a mask of concern. "If I had known you were here, I could have—"

"Save it, Lucian!" Mother snapped. "I don't recall issuing you an invitation to enter my home when you pleased. I suggest you take your Spark and your person and head back to the Palace, or wherever you make your domicile these days."

Lucian scowled. "I merely came here to inform Her Majesty that she is due for a ride in the countryside with the

Mayor of Seacliff this afternoon, and to ask if she wished to indulge him this day, or if it were otherwise and she has…other matters….which demand her attention."

"She will be occupied for the rest of the day", the Queen replied crisply. "Thank you, Lucian, you may go."
Lucian glanced at my mother—both my mothers—with a strange searching expression before bowing stiffly and murmuring a "Of course, Your Majesty. Come, Spark."

The flamemaid named Spark took one last look around. I heard Leaf draw in a sharp breath, and for a moment I entertained the absurd notion that Spark could smell Leaf and knew that someone else was there besides Queen and Council.

Fortunately, to Leaf's visible relief, the flamemaid simply turned to follow her bondmate out the door without looking back. Once again, silence reigned for the space of several heartbeats, and then mother and Queen let out simultaneous sighs of relief, mother gesturing for me to leave my hiding place.

"That was Lucian," my mother explained. "Known as the Lion General, an excellent soldier, back in the day."

"He still is," the Queen remarked. "But he is not the man he once was, that's for certain."
"Why is everyone so frightened of him, mother?" I asked.
Mother was silent for a long time. "Because he's an ambitious man, Hedda," she said finally, "and that ambition makes him dangerous."

The Queen nodded in agreement. "Were it not for me," she said, frowning. "Perhaps he would not be so ambitious."
Mother shook her head. "It's hardly your fault, Sofiya."

The Queen smiled. "You are ever ready to defend me, Augusta, but that is the truth of the matter."

My mother took her hands and kissed them. "And you,

apparently, have been risking the lives of good people to look after me," she nodded towards her study. "You sent Kainet to watch us, didn't you?"

The Queen shrugged, but she was smiling slyly. "I might have," she said. "You can never be too careful out in the country, Augusta."

Mother snorted. "I managed for a great many years," she remarked, reaching over to stroke the Queen's cheek. "But, I have to admit, the worst part about living out there was that you weren't in my life."

"Charmer," the Queen chuckled. "In any case, I'd better go consult with my spies regarding Lucian's latest plot to kill me…." She spoke so casually that one might have imagined she was discussing the weather. In fact, I wasn't sure if it was just an extremely macabre joke.

I couldn't hold it in anymore.

"Um, excuse me," I said, wary of interrupting them.

They both turned to me. "What is it, Hedda?" Mother asked.

I coughed to clear my throat; then locked gazes with the Queen. "If everyone's so afraid of him and he tried to kill you," I began. "Why don't you just kill him? Everyone keeps telling me that people who bond to elder spirits make competent assassins; why not just hire one of them?"

"Ah, Hedda, considering a career in less lawful forms of employment, are we?" The Queen teased, coming over to me and taking my hands in hers.

"A good question," she said. "The answer is, regrettably, complicated, politics, mostly, and matters of honour. I won't be like monarchs past, poisoning everyone who poses the slightest threat to me or my family. Regarding Lucian in particular, it is a long story."

I hope we get to hear the whole story eventually, Leaf remarked. *I suppose it's one more thing we won't know until we need to know.*

It seems like everything is on a 'need to know' basis, I agreed. Turning my attention back to the Queen—I still couldn't believe that I had two mothers—and nodded to show that I understood. She nodded in return, giving me a brilliant smile before turning back to my mother.

"Can you stay at all, or do you need to be back at the Palace with Princess Luccia?" Mother asked.

The Queen shook her head. "Luccia is well-guarded," she said. "And I have a half-dozen wind spirits ready to relay messages to any number of guards should an attempt on her life be made. It would be much easier if I had bonded myself. If the royal family did not traditionally abstain from bonding with spirits, perhaps….perhaps things would be different…." She glanced over at me. "Perhaps everything would be different."

Mother rested a hand on her shoulder. "There are some things you can't change, Sofiya," and then her expression turned impish. "Come on, let's go find some way to distract you from all these dark thoughts."

Sofiya grinned. "I can think of a couple ways," she said. "But, ah, perhaps not in front of your daughter."

"*Our* daughter," mother corrected, her hand trailing down the Queen's arm until she grasped her hand. .

The Queen sighed. "I only wish it could have always been so, none of this hiding and having to keep up appearances."

"We'll get through this," mother promised, grasping the Queen's hand tightly. She turned to me, grinning, "Right Hedda? Leaf?"

"Right!" we chorused.

"There, you see?" Mother said to the Queen. "Everything

123

will be fine, Sofiya."

"I don't think it will be that easy," said Sofiya. "But, one can only hope that you turn out to be right."

To my great surprise, the Queen actually supped with us. The servants made a predictable fuss over it, of course, and Ser Palverel nearly lost his wits when he heard the news. As the only person bonded to an eldermaid, I was permitted to taste the Queen's food before it was set at her place. After pronouncing it safe to eat, we all sat down to supper. The Queen was a great storyteller, and would tell us all of the misadventures of various courtiers in the years when mother was away from court.

"Do you remember Ser Latis and Ser Kells?" she asked my mother. "The two of them broke plenty of hearts in the court as young men, but once they found each other, they only broke their own hearts, over and over."

"I remember them," mother said, smiling fondly. "They were both enthusiastic worshipers of the Sadist, unless I'm recalling a different couple?"

The Queen shook her head. "No, the very same, although many are perhaps less public about that particular sport as those two. In any case, they are married now, I don't think I've ever seen them happier, to be honest."

"Who are they talking about?" I whispered to Sebastian. Sebastian grinned. "The Royal Falconer and the current Head of the Order of Sudrask, respectively, both trusted advisors to the Queen on matters of birds and the acquisition of knowledge and technology."

"Ah," I said. My mother had not taken me to see the Great Library of Firehaven, which was built during an age of scholastic zeal. I would have gone myself, but, truth be told, I wasn't sure how Leaf would react to seeing so much paper in one place, although she had been mildly curious about individual books. I supposed that spirits really had no use for such things, as their knowledge is kept in their heads. *Hedda, by "sport", I suppose the Queen isn't referring to activities involving a ball and a net? Well, maybe more than one ball, in this case.*

I almost spat out my soup, and instead made a very undignified choking sound. *Leaf! Stop sending, now!*

Mother turned from her discussion with the Queen to regard me. "Are you well, Hedda?" she asked.

"I'm fine," I managed to gasp out. "I just—Leaf—startled me a bit....that's all...."

Mother returned to her conversation. I gave Leaf a pointed look; then dipped my spoon in the soup again. Ser Palverel had prepared chicken soup with lentils. It was one of those dishes that smelled horrible until you began to eat it, and then you realized that it really wasn't that bad after all.

When everyone finished eating the soup, the main course was brought out. Ser Palverel had apparently decided that roast duck in orange sauce was a fitting main course for a visiting monarch, and it was very good, even though I didn't particularly like duck. Ser Palverel himself brought out desert, it was a fluffy cake piled with cream whipped so finely that it looked like clouds, which he presented to the Queen with a flourish, while apologizing for such meager fare. The Queen merely laughed at this and gestured for everyone to take a share.

I liked dessert most of all.

After we supped, everyone sat around the hearth fire, because there were still more stories to tell, and then, when everyone had exhausted their store of tales, mother gently touched the Queen's arm, bid Leaf, Ember, and I good night, and went up to bed side by side with her monarch—her lover.

As I lay in my bed that night, I wished that all our days could be similar to this one, where we didn't have to worry about plotting and scheming.

CHAPTER TWELVE

Kamalak summoned Leaf and I to His lair the next day. I went expecting to fight more of His shadows, as this had become routine since the two of us began training with Him, but to my surprise, I found Him sitting on His throne alone. Usually, He was attended at all times by metalmaids, at least, but this time, a strange silence permeated the God of Thieves' Court.

"Where is everyone?" I asked as I entered. The hoard of treasure was still there, so I didn't think they were moving, but neither was there any hint of movement, no sign that anyone was there besides myself, Leaf, and the Son of Ilisith.

"Out," He said simply, rising from His seat and gesturing to a nearby crate. "Sit," He commanded. "We have much to discuss...."

I sat down, gesturing for Leaf to sit beside me. The last

time Kamalak had said those words, it hadn't ended well for us. Well, since my life was about to take an unpleasant turn, I thought I might as well take the initiative and ask the one question that had been on my mind since I'd learned about my royal mother.

"Why didn't You tell me?" I blurted out.

"Why didn't I tell you what, dearest Hedda?" Kamalak cooed, smiling that knife smile that said he damned well knew what I was going to say. I had never wanted to smack someone as much as I wanted to smack the god at that moment, but that would have been fatally stupid, so I only scowled.

"Why didn't You tell me that the Queen is my mother?" I clarified.

Kamalak's smile broadened. "I can't possibly keep track of every mortal's parentage, dearest Hedda. You would have to look to My Father for that. Oh, but He is gone, is He not? More's the pity." He sat back down on the throne with an audible thump. "Do you truly wish to know why?"

I almost said no, for, like most answers from the god, I suspected that I did not wish to hear this one, but in the end, my desire for answers won out over my apprehension.

"Tell me," I urged—no, more like begged—Him. "Why didn't You tell me?"

Kamalak leaned forward, and even though I would not have been close enough to smell His breath had He been human, that was what I smelled now. He smelled of incense and candle wax, of the deep night with no stars. The stars behind His eyes burst as He spoke. "I did not tell you, because then you would have been of no use to Me…."

Well, that wasn't the answer I was expecting to hear from Him. "Why?"

Kamalak sat back and regarded me with half-lidded eyes.

"'Tis simple, dearest Hedda," He began. "You would not have been the sort of person that I needed for my little movement." There it was again, that knife-smile . "I needed someone who did not yet have her head stuffed full of flights of fancy that she could not empathize with the plight of My people."

"But—" I bit my lip. "I'm sure there were—there are—nobles who could have been just as much, if not more helpful than Leaf and I--"

"No, Hedda," said Kamalak. "Ah, you truly do not understand your place in this great tapestry, but I suppose that is how it is with mortals, always living out their lives blissfully unaware of the roles they play, never knowing if history will remember them or if they will become dust in the wind, and so it was, dust and wind, and then, one day, someone brings with them an opportunity for change."

I had wanted answers, but this, I wasn't sure how to respond to this. "But why not just maneuver things so that one of Your thieves could be the instrument of change?" I asked. "Why wait for an opportunity that might never come, instead of acting?"

Kamalak smiled mysteriously. "You are acting as if you are the catalyst in a solution, and the rest of us were merely waiting for you, like a promised savior!" His smile widened. "Ha! Do you still fill your head with those old tales? They become so boring after awhile." He shook His head. "No, Hedda, you are not a catalyst, you are merely a missing part in a well-crafted mechanism, like the serpent lock on the door leading to this chamber. Perhaps you are its fang or its eye, but no less, and no more important than every other piece, and you may not—in fact, it is safe to say that you are not—even the most important piece in the machine. The machine only works properly when all the parts are together."

So saying, He knitted His fingers together, then folded His hands and rested them on His lap, smiling his cat-smile this time. "Do you understand, child?"

"I—I think so." I replied. When He put it that way, it made sense. "So, is that why all of them are gone? They're preparing for something?" A sudden pang of fear went through me.

General Lucian! It could only be him. Who else could it be? Even the Queen had admitted that he had tried to kill her. "Is he—is General Lucian about to do something?!"
I never thought I would have ever seen one of the Powers do it, but the God of Luck shrugged.

"The winds of change are moving in many different directions," He mused. "It is difficult—even for one of the Powers, to predict which way they may blow."

"You didn't answer my question," I pointed out, but He just ignored me, reaching out and picking up His sword, which leaned against His throne.

"But enough of this," He murmured as he rose and pointed the sword at me. "Come, children! This will be your last lesson; we might as well make sure it counts."

I wasn't sure how long I fought with the god, was even less certain of the number of times He knocked me down nor of the number of times He deflected Leaf's attacks. It had taken us so long to learn how to fight as one, but now we moved together, stretching the bond between us to its limits as we planned out avenues of attack; it was almost as if Leaf was an extension of me, and I of her. I remembered how Igraine and Nut had worked together all those years ago and how I had wished that I and Leaf could have that sort of connection.

Now I did not have to wish, I knew now what it felt like

to be in complete accord with one's bondmate.

Leaf! To your left!

Hedda, duck!

That was why I could not resist grinning when Leaf struck Kamalak and the god actually staggered half a step back, His hand flying to His cheek, where a line of pale ichor had appeared. As quickly as it had come, however, it disappeared.

It's likely He allowed us to hit Him, you know? Leaf said.

I know, I replied. *I can't help but grin though, can you?*

No, she admitted, and grinned.

Kamalak's head was bowed as if in prayer, but then He slowly began to clap,

"Well done," He praised, and I felt that if I only received those two words of praise in my entire life, I could die knowing I had accomplished the impossible.

"Well done indeed," He repeated, his expression turning thoughtful. "I am thus reassured that if you happen to die in the coming days, it will not be because I—nor any of your other teachers—have not trained you well."

My eyes widened, fear suddenly seizing me, but He merely clapped a hand on my shoulder and grinned, leaning close to whisper in my ear.

"Try not to die in the coming days, child," He said. "It would reflect badly on Me, and I would rather not lose another piece in this mechanism if I can help it." He gazed up at the ceiling, a faraway look in His eyes.

"Events are already in motion," He murmured. "The tapestry is already being woven; I wonder…"—and here He stroked His chin thoughtfully—"….what image will be produced when the weaving is finished?"

And with that, He went to sit on His throne again, almost as if He had never left it, and dismissed us with a wave of His hand.

"Farewell, child," He said. "Perhaps you will see Me when this is all over, but if not, I promise not to steal anything off your corpse!" And then He laughed at His own macabre sentiment, a strange, wild sound, that laughter of the God of Thieves.

"They say that you can hear the laughter of the God of Thieves in alleyways at night," I said to Leaf as we passed through the serpent door. "Now that I have actually heard it, I can say with confidence that it's true."

"I wonder how much of what 'they' say is true is really true," Leaf mused.

I shrugged. "I don't know. Maybe most of it is only partially true, who really knows but the Powers Themselves?"

"I suppose you're right," said Leaf, and then she stopped suddenly, glancing around. "Hedda?"

"What is it, Leaf?"

"He didn't send us back with a guide this time…"

I felt a pang of fear slice through me; but then I stopped to consider Kamalak's words from earlier, grinning up at the elder spirit.

"We don't need a guide anymore, Leaf," I said as I quickened my steps. "We can find our own way home now!"

I was right, we found our way back in no time, literally, considering how slowly time passed here compared to when we were with Kamalak. Instead of heading straight home though, as we usually did, we stopped at the market to spend a little coin on sweet cakes drizzled with honey and sprinkled with crushed almonds. For Leaf, I bought her a treat of fresh water from the mountain springs that were north of Firehaven, said to have healing properties for those who drank or bathed in the waters. It was said that one could find many different spirits residing in or near those springs, but that no one spirit had claim to the land there.

"I can understand why they would find the springs so attractive," Leaf remarked. "The water they produce is delicious!"

"I'm glad you like it," I said, in between mouthfuls of honey cake. I had made certain to buy a few extra to share with mother and whoever else would like one. "Leaf?"

"Yes, Hedda?"

"What do you think will happen to us, after…considering everything that's happened?"

Leaf set her bucket of water down and shrugged. "I don't know, I still don't completely understand human politics." She paused, a thoughtful expression on her face. "But…surely the Queen wouldn't want Augusta to be unhappy, so I imagine that she will do what she thinks will keep you both happy."

"And you and Ember," I added.

"Yes, that's right," she affirmed, dipping her roots into the bucket and sighing.

I felt a little better, hearing Leaf's words, and unlike many other nations, ours did not mandate that the first-born child should inherit the throne, so I did not worry that I would be asked to assume a position of authority when I had had no training in statecraft—undoubtedly another reason that my mother had avoided taking me to the city for so long—besides, Princess Luccia had practically been born on a throne, and so would have little trouble taking on that mantle when the Queen decided to abdicate….

….*Or in the event of her death.* I thought grimly, and then I was back to thinking about Kamalak's words again. He had said that I only had a couple days, and I trusted the word of a god—even the God of Thieves, over anything anyone else might tell me about what was going on in the Palace.

"Leaf," I said as I carefully folded the paper bag closed. "I think we need to go home, and we need to train as hard as ever. If Kamalak is right, I don't want to take any chances...." *And if He was wrong or joking, well, then we'll just look like fools.* I wasn't willing to wager against a god's word, however; especially not when that god is also the God of Luck.

It seemed a little absurd, but I sent up a quick prayer to Him. *If You were telling the truth about what will happen in a couple days time, grant me Luck in the days ahead,* I prayed.

And then, I felt something I had not felt in many years. I could have sworn it felt as if Someone was listening.

CHAPTER THIRTEEN

We spent the rest of the day practicing all that we knew. We reviewed everything our many mentors had taught us over the years. I saw mother briefly; she appeared harried, as if she had not slept very much last night. When I asked Sebastian what was wrong, he just said "matters of intelligence," and left it at that.

It wasn't just mother; though, all of the household staff were on edge. In fact, the entire city seemed on edge, as if it was collectively holding its breath. I had barely noticed it at the market, but now that I stopped to consider it, it did seem strange how there were so few people about. Even the temples, usually centers of tranquility, seemed a little out of sorts. Once again, I turned to Sebastian for news, and this time, he readily provided it.

"I heard that the savants of Ilisith gave quite the substantial offering to the Sadist last night," he said.

I swallowed nervously. The Sadist is the aspect of Ilisith most closely aligned with War—as much as Love can be aligned with War—and is often invoked to protect the temple and its savants from assault from within and without. He is also the only one of His aspects who receives offerings of blood, not sacrifices—none of the Powers require ritual slaughter—but offerings, large or small.

"Do they have a reason to be concerned?" I asked, though I suspected I already knew the answer.

Sebastian frowned. "There have been whispers, of course, there always are, and many believe that it is best to be cautious in the coming days. Rarely does the savantry make an offering on such a grand scale to the Sadist if there is no concern for the safety of the Order, apart from certain festival days, of course."

"I would do the same thing, were I them, I think," Leaf chimed in. "Even if the Powers are not listening, perhaps it will put minds at ease, knowing that the ritual has been performed properly."

I frowned. "Or it could merely make people more anxious…." I knew that there were many who said that the Powers had never existed in the first place, that They were merely stories that our ancestors wove to understand things that they could not yet comprehend.

Sebastian gave us a reassuring smile with just a hint of sadness to it. "Come what may, we can only be as ready as we can be, and hope for the best."

It was reassuring that Sebastian was able to maintain his boundless optimism when everyone around us seemed to be preparing for the inevitable, and so I found myself smiling back. "Well, Leaf and I will be as ready as we can be, that's a promise."

"Good," said Sebastian. "I'll hold you to that promise."

That night, as we headed up to bed after a long day of training, Leaf turned to me and said "You really shouldn't make promises you can't keep, Hedda."

"That's why I'm going to keep my promise," I replied. Leaf grinned. "And when it's time to keep your promise, I'll be right there beside you." She took my hand and squeezed it, and I felt the part of her, the splinter that was beneath my skin, flare with warmth for a brief moment.

"Always," she finished, her grin broadening.

"Always," I agreed.

The next day, we were all surprised when the Queen came calling.

"We're all going riding today!" She announced, gesturing for two grooms to approach leading horses for mother and I. They were fine animals: one a dark chestnut, the other the colour of cream. The Queen's horse was black, and glared at everyone assembled in the courtyard as if we were personally responsible for making him wait until he was allowed to run again.

My mother didn't seem too pleased with the suggestion. "Sofiya, everyone is on edge as it is. Should you really be heading out at this time? The people need their Queen." The Queen's smile vanished, her lips drawing into a hard line as she firmly shook her head.

"They need to see that I am up and about, Augusta." She stated. "I refuse to be intimidated by him, so I will ride with my daughters and one of my best generals, and all will be well." She gestured to someone I couldn't see. "Come, Luccia, there's someone I would like you to meet."

The girl who came to stand at the Queen's side was almost the mirror image of her mother, with the same brown skin and dark hair, but her eyes were bright green, in contrast to her mother's warm brown. She appeared to be younger than me, though we were the same height.

"Luccia, this is Hedda and her bondmate, Leaf," said the Queen. "I have been waiting a long time for this meeting."

"Pleased to meet you, Hedda, Leaf," said Luccia, smiling shyly. *This is my sister,* I thought as I returned her smile with a nervous one of my own. "Pleased to meet you, Pr—"

"—Luccia," she interrupted. "I'm just Luccia to you; enough people call me 'Princess' all the time." She took my hand and led me to where her horse, a palomino, stood patiently waiting for her.

"This is Sunfire," she said as she rested a hand on the horse's muzzle. "Mother gave her to me last year for my birthday. Isn't she wonderful?"

"She is," I agreed, reaching up to pet her, as Leaf examined her curiously. She was always so fascinated by animals, my bondmate, few spirits are as close to the land as the spirits of the trees.

"I still do not understand how they manage to tolerate carrying all that weight," she remarked to me offhandedly, gesturing to the horse's tack. "If I had to wear all of that for most of the day, I do not think I would enjoy it so much."

"Don't worry, Leaf," I said. "I'm sure the Palace staff takes good care of the horses."

"Oh yes," Luccia agreed. "No one would ever dream of overburdening any of them!" She glanced up at Leaf, wonder in her eyes.

"What's it like, being bonded to a spirit?" She asked.

"Mother says that traditionally, the royal family doesn't bond with spirits. I suppose yours didn't know that when she bonded with you."

"I didn't know either," I admitted, reminded of the fact that I wasn't simply Hedda anymore, but a princess, even though the girl standing before me would be the one to occupy the throne. "I don't think we could have helped it if we had known. Spirits bond to whomever they wish, after all, and no rules that humans make will ever change that fact."

Leaf was nodding her head in agreement. Luccia looked thoughtful.

"Well, I suppose I shall keep an open mind, then," she said at last, giving me a smile before she mounted her horse. "Are you coming for a ride?" She asked. "Mother had the grooms fix up Moonglow for you...."

I glanced at my mother, who was still scowling. "Mother?"

My mother sighed, resigned to her fate. "Fine, we'll all go riding!" She snarled as she swung up into the chestnut's saddle like someone who had spent many years in it. "Slowly, though," she warned. "Hedda is not accustomed to riding." "Slowly," the Queen repeated as I was helped up into the saddle by one of the grooms.

"Is it okay if Leaf runs alongside us?" I asked.

The Queen glanced at my bondmate. "We usually discourage spirits from running alongside the horses, but in this case, I don't see why not, as long as she doesn't make any sudden movements."

"Of course," I said, nodding to Leaf. *You heard her,* I sent. *No sudden movements.*

Relax, Hedda, Leaf assured me. *I'll be careful not to spook the horses. Nightchaser has said that he will not bite me if I don't come too close to him.*

Nightchaser? I glanced over at the Queen's horse. He was glaring at us, no, at Leaf in particular.

You can understand horses? I asked.

Oh yes, said Leaf. *You....hadn't noticed, after all this time?*

I shook my head. *It just never occurred to me.* I admitted.

Leaf shrugged. *Horses do not generally have much to say to anyone who isn't a horse, anyways, and that includes spirits.*

I was about to reply but the Queen made a clucking sound with her tongue and Nightdancer began to move. The rest of us followed in their wake. I was nervous at first, for I wasn't used to how Moonglow shifted as we moved, but was reassured by Leaf's constant presence at the horse's side.

Someone drew up on my other side, and when I glanced over, I was surprised to see Kainet.

"Hello, Princess," he said by way of greeting—it was so strange, being called "Princess" all of a sudden—and nodding to Leaf. He was astride a bay horse, and, like Leaf, Seed walked at his side.

"Hello, Ser Kainet," I said in greeting. "It's been a long time. What are you doing here?" I had an idea of what he was doing here, but I wanted to hear him say it.

Kainet grinned. "I'm just here to make sure nothing befalls the royal family as they enjoy their afternoon ride."

"Is that why you were spying on us all these years, Kainet?" My mother called from where she rode up front with the Queen.

"Ah, Lady Augusta, protecting the royal family has been my job from the start, that includes you, you know, even if I had to be more....circumspect....in doing it." He turned his attention back to me. "Such is the life of the Queen's Spymaster."

"Queen's Spymaster?" I narrowed my eyes at him. "You seem a little—"

Kainet grinned. "—A little young to be a Spymaster? You and most of the court seem to think so…." He turned his attention to the two women riding ahead of us, their heads close together in conversation. Mother laughed about something the Queen said, and I saw Kainet smile fondly at the pair.

"Hi, Hedda!" Luccia chirped as she came up on my other side. She took a deep breath of the cool air. "Isn't it a great day for riding?"

To be honest, I didn't really know what was considered a good day for riding, but it was a warm autumn day so I smiled and nodded. "It certainly is a nice day."

Luccia grinned. "Is Moonglow being kind to you? I told her she couldn't make a fuss while you were riding her."

"I think she's doing fine," I replied, hesitantly reaching out and stroking her neck. "I think it's more me that needs to become accustomed to her!"

"I forget that you didn't have the tutors I had," Luccia remarked. "Mother has told me so much about you, you know?"

"Has she?"

She nodded. "I've always wanted a sister, but my mother always said that she wasn't planning to have more children, and then, one day she told me about you." Her expression grew wistful. "I remember how I wanted to muster a army to bring you to Firehaven, but mother said that we couldn't, that you and your mother had to stay away for a time." She looked away. "I didn't understand what she meant at the time, but now…." She looked up at me, and then she gave me a smile that was like the sun coming out after days of rain. "You're here now, that's what matters!" She reached over, Leaf drawing back out of her way, and placed a hand atop mine.

I nodded. "And I don't think any of us will be going away, not after all that's happened…"

"I hope so," she said.

Hedda! Duck!

I heard Leaf's warning and shouted for Luccia to duck, pressing myself flat against Moonglow, feeling the air move as an arrow whizzed by out heads.

Several things happened at once.

Luccia screamed, pulling hard on the reins, causing Sunfire to nearly bolt. Kainet went to help Luccia, and mother and the Queen drew their swords, alert and already scanning the area. Leaf and Seed, on the other hand, promptly vanished into the woods in pursuit of the assailant.

"Stay alert, everyone," mother warned. "For all we know, there could be more than one."

Leaf and Seed returned a moment later, Seed dragging the limp form of a man.

"We caught up to him, but by that time—" Leaf glanced at the man. "—It was too late…"

"Poison?" mother asked.

Leaf nodded. "I'm sorry, I—I couldn't do anything…."

"It's okay, Leaf," I reassured her. "It wasn't your fault. You couldn't have known."

Kainet dismounted to help Seed carry the body away, Leaf staring after them until they were out of sight. I tried my best to put the image out of my mind. I had seen dead animals before, as mother often hunted for our supper, but never dead humans. It occurred to me that Leaf might be even more sensitive to such things, and upon taking her hand; I could feel that she was trembling. I began to gently rub the back of it with my thumb.

"There there now, Leaf; he poisoned himself. There is nothing you could have done," I said. "And if you had not warned me, I would probably be dead as well."

Leaf looked up at me, sap running down her cheeks. "Really?" she squeaked.

"Really," I said. "Right, Luccia?"

"I think she saved us both," Luccia said. "I lost a little hair, but that's paltry compared to what I might have lost had he been aiming for me." She lowered her voice. "Do you think Lucian sent him?"

General Lucian seemed like the obvious culprit, but I was hesitant to place all the blame on him, especially after what Kamalak had said during one of my lessons, about how the Queen turned a blind eye to the plight of the common people. It was a sentiment that seemed so at odds with the woman I knew, who had been nothing but kind to me, but sometimes, as I was to learn, as I had already seen, the faces we show in public were different than the ones we showed in private. "I don't know," I said at last. "I suppose he might have, especially with the way everyone's been talking about him. I just don't understand why your mother doesn't just get rid of him, if he's so troublesome."

Luccia shrugged. "It may not look it to you, but there are some things that you must do as Queen that can be very hard, indeed, although there are many benefits to being the one on the throne. Tradition, obligation, honor...." She sighed. "Sometimes I wonder if mother doesn't feel as if she's in thrall to the court's whims instead of the other way round, and is either really preferable? "

That was an interesting way of looking at it, but I didn't have much time to ponder it before Kainet returned with Seed and went to confer with the Queen.

"I asked the Queen of the Forest to open the ground for me; then I tossed him in." He reported. "He's in Yemena's hands now."

The Queen nodded gravely; then lightly flicked Nightchaser's reins. "Let's continue on," she said decisively, drawing herself up in the saddle.

"Are you certain, Sofiya?" Mother asked; concern in her voice.

The Queen drew herself up in the saddle so that she sat straight and tall. "I cannot appear to have been cowed, Augusta, that is what he wants."

"Assuming that he was the one who ordered the attack," said Kainet.

"Even so, I cannot afford to look as if I've been shaken by this," said the Queen. "The people need to see that their Queen is capable of withstanding anything." She gave him a sad smile. "I need all the support I can get, Kainet, if we are to weather this storm."

"I understand, but—" Kainet glanced up at the sky. "I can't help but feel that there's a better way to resolve all this...."

All of a sudden, a great gust of wind sent the fallen leaves around us into a wild frenzy. The cold wind crept under my cloak and chilled me. Luccia's dark hair was like a big black banner, while Kainet was once again gazing upward at the sky. I followed the Spymaster's gaze, and, to my astonishment, I saw figures darting around in the sky. They were hard to see at first, but the longer I watched them, the more I found that I was capable of making them out. I recalled the Queen talking about wind spirits. I had never seen one before, of course, I had never known where to look to find one.

Kainet swore viciously. "The wind spirits!" He cried. " They wouldn't be this agitated unless something's amiss in Firehaven!" He quickly turned his horse, spurring him into a gallop.

"We need to go!" Mother exclaimed, turning her horse as well. "Leaf, support Hedda so that she doesn't fall off her horse, we need to move quickly!"

Leaf nodded, and before I could say anything, she wrapped her arms around me, her legs stretching into branches which wrapped around the horse's underbelly, holding me steady in a secure enclosure that wouldn't hinder the horse's movement.

"Hold on tight, Hedda!" Mother cried, coming up alongside Moonglow. "You won't fall off while Leaf has you, but it's going to be bumpy," and, so saying, she slapped the horse's rump, yelling at her to go.

Moonglow surged forward, and for few panicked moments I imagined that I was going to fall off regardless of Leaf's assistance, but the eldermaid's grip held even as we bounded over fallen logs that we had merely stepped over a moment ago. The forest was a blur of red, orange, and yellow as we passed, and I had to force myself to look straight ahead so that nausea wouldn't overtake me.

You're doing great, Hedda. Leaf said encouragingly, but suddenly I felt her concern.

Oh, wait, who is that in the road?

The others had stopped at the entrance to the forest, and they faced a row of people in dark red armor: members of the Order of Menaishe, all on foot. I brought Moonglow to a halt beside Luccia.

"What's going on?!" I hissed.

Luccia glanced at me, a worried expression on her face.

"They just suddenly appeared," she whispered. "I don't know just what they want, but it doesn't seem like they want anything good."

Still astride Nightchaser, the Queen approached the line of soldiers.

"Let us pass!" She ordered, sounding like a Queen should sound: confident, in charge.

One of the soldiers stepped forward. "I'm sorry, Your Majesty," she said, and then the entire row drew their swords.

Something occurred to me, then.

Leaf, have any of them bonded? I asked.

I don't sense any—

"--Everybody move! Now!"

Kainet's voice was so full of urgency that I didn't bother to question it, just dug my heels into Moonglow and held on tightly. The ground before me erupted in flames. I thought I heard Luccia scream, but I couldn't see much of anything through the ash and smoke that suddenly covered the ground. I heard someone else scream, and the unmistakable scent of burning flesh assaulted my nostrils.

All of a sudden, Kainet was there beside me. "Keep moving!" He shouted. "Get to the Temple of Kinarshe, you should be safe there!"

"Where's my mother?" I cried. "Where are both my mothers?!"

"Don't worry about them, they can handle themselves!" He assured me. "Now get moving, and in the name of the Powers, stay alive!"

Suddenly, I could see clearly again, but I did not think to look back, only pressed forward as I'd been told. There were no soldiers in my path now; I could only assume that they were otherwise engaged.

"Hedda!"

I bit back a cry of relief when I heard Luccia's voice, but when I turned towards her, I saw that she was being pursued, not by any of the soldiers—none of them could have outran Sunfire, but by a flamemaid, most likely one bonded to one of those soldiers.

"Hedda!" Luccia cried again, narrowly dodging out of the way of a fireball the spirit threw. "Help me!"

I didn't have time to think of a better way to help her. "Leaf, go!" I shouted.

I watched as the treemaid charged the flamemaid, lifting a rock that was easily the size of my head and flinging it at her. The fire spirit was so distracted by Luccia that she didn't notice Leaf or the rock until the rock slammed into her, knocking her to the ground. I held onto Moonglow for dear life, now that Leaf was no longer there to support me. Leaf had snatched up another rock and was ready to fling it at her again. She would not attack an opponent while they were down.

The flamemaid sprang to her feet, the wreath of flames around her head blazing with her anger. The first rock had only stunned her momentarily, not disabled her, and now Leaf was truly in danger. I couldn't tear my eyes away as the flamemaid advanced on my eldermaid, my heart in my throat. I wanted to call out to her, and found that I couldn't get the breath to form words.

A sudden gust of wind blew my hair into my eyes, and then the most amazing thing happened.

A windjack tore through the flamemaid in a way that would have killed a human, bursting through her chest. Leaf was thrown back as more wind spirits appeared, surrounding the flamemaid, rapidly circling her. As I watched, the flamemaid crumpled to the ground, and then, just like that, she was gone, snuffed out like a candle flame. Their grim task completed, the wind spirits dispersed, each moving in a different direction.

Luccia trotted over to me. her knuckles white as she clutched Sunfire's reins. "What happened? Where--where did she go?"

I glanced at the spot where the wind spirits had been. "Mother told me once that flamemaids are dependent on air for their survival. I think—I think it's like using a candle snuffer."

"What happens to her…."

"Her bonded? I don't know." I replied. "Mother told me once that it's very painful, suddenly losing your bondmate, and some are driven to the point of suicide. She also said that the spirit is never truly destroyed though, that they just return in another form."

"How?"

I shrugged. "Who knows how spirits truly work, apart from the Powers Themselves?" I glanced over at Leaf, who was just now making her way towards us. "Leaf, are you okay?"

Leaf nodded. "I'm fine….I remembered that Kainet had seen the wind spirits before, so I called to them. It's a good thing they heard me in time, or I…."

I held up a hand to stop her from finishing that sentence. "Don't say anything, Leaf," I said. "The important thing is that you're here." I turned to Luccia. "Sir Kainet told me to head to the Temple of Kinarshe, you should come with us."

Luccia was silent for a few moments, and then she nodded agreement. "I don't think it would be safe for me back at the Palace, members of the Order of Menaishe are everywhere, and after what just occurred…." She glanced down at her hands, then back up at me, and steel flashed in her eyes for the barest of moments. "I won't let him win, Hedda!"

"Neither will I," I replied, gathering Moonglow's reins in my hands. "Let's head to the Temple of Kinarshe, we can talk about where to go from there."

CHAPTER FOURTEEN

We never made it to the Temple of Kinarshe.

The city was in chaos when we arrived. People and spirits were running to and fro, and there were so many voices talking at once that I couldn't even begin to piece together what was going on.

"Princess!"

I turned to see Savant Chesnos running towards us, my delight at seeing a familiar face quickly turned to concern as he came closer. His yellow robes were tattered and covered in ash and soot. One of his eye eyes was blackened, but otherwise he appeared to be undamaged.

"Savant Chesnos! What happened to you?" I asked as he came to a halt before the horses.

"It's....the temple!" Chesnos gasped. "You need to come quickly! I think General Lucian has gone mad!"

"What has happened?" Luccia demanded. "Why are the

people in such a panic?"

Chesnos looked down at the ground, shaking his head as if he didn't know where to begin.

"It all started this morning," he began. "The Queen departed and General Lucian began sending guards out into the streets. There's rioting, the Old City is in chaos, and—" and here his voice broke, his whole body shook, whether with rage, despair, or both, I could not tell.

He looked up at us, and I could see rage burning in his eyes. "Now he's at the temple, saying how the Savantry of Ilisith is responsible for the Queen putting him aside. The Head of the Order is trying to reason with him, but I fear he's lost the ability to see reason. You must come, and quickly!"

I glanced at Luccia, her mouth was set in a firm line. "We will come with you," she said, dismounting. "Come on, Hedda, leave the horses here. If General Lucian is really this unstable, we might need to fight, and the horses will only get hurt if it turns into a melee.

"Good idea," I swung my leg up over the saddle and dismounted, tying the reins to a nearby post, there wasn't much we could do if they were stolen, but it was the best we could do, given the circumstances.

"Let's go," said Luccia. "If we get there fast enough, maybe the temple will still be standing."

"I hope so," I said earnestly. *Leaf,* I sent. *Be ready for anything, okay?*

I can't promise that I'll be ready for everything, Leaf sent back. *But I will be ready in case there's a fight. I'll protect both of you!*

That's all any of us can ask, Leaf, I sent back. *Whatever happens, though, we're in this together.*

Always, said Leaf.

And with that, we set our sights on the Temple of Ilisith.

I prayed that we were not too late.

A crowd was gathered before the Temple of Ilisith. Before the doors to the temple, members of the Order of Menaishe stood guard. Off to the side stood a knot of the temple's savants, also under guard. I thought I could see the old man who welcomed me to the temple on the day of my first moonblood. He was slumped over, and at first I feared he was dead, but as I came closer, I saw that his lips were moving in a silent prayer. I couldn't see Adebayo anywhere. I wondered if perhaps he had not taken his vows after all, and had left the city long before this mess with General Lucian, or perhaps he had returned to Lord Kamalak's employ. Wherever he was, I wished him well.

In the centre of the chaos was General Lucian, of course, who stood with some of Menaishe's Order before the doors of the temple. He was arguing loudly with someone; and as Luccia and I drew nearer, I saw that he was arguing with the Grandmistress of the Order of Menaishe herself.

"—need to stop this madness, Lucian!" Grandmistress Yehmina was snarling, a naked sword in her hands. "You have committed enough acts of treason and sacrilege today! It ends now, in front of these witnesses!" She raised her sword, pointing it straight at his throat. "Step down from there," she ordered. "*Now....* "

Lucian seemed unconcerned with the naked blade that was pointed at him. "No, Yehmina, I don't think I will," he replied silkily, beginning to pace. Yehmina followed him with her eyes, but her blade didn't waver.

"I need to do what I must to protect this city, after all," he continued, leering at her. "That is one part of your job that you have been sorely neglecting, my dear."

Yehmina spat on the ground, "That is what I think of your 'protection', Lucian!" She cried. "The people of the Old City, were they not worthy of your protection?!"

Lucian glanced up at her, and then he smiled, the same sort of knife smile Kamalak would give me during our meetings, only this one seemed considerably more malicious. "Don't concern yourself with a small riot over the price of food," he said, completely unconcerned. "Why do you care so much, Yehmina? It's not as if you or your soldiers ever even glanced in the direction of the Old City. Do you even know where it is?"

I watched as Yehmina's jaw clenched in obvious anger, but the words that came out of her mouth were spoken in a calm, even tone.

"I have sworn to protect all the people of Firehaven from anything that poses a threat to their wellbeing." She declared. "You claim I do not care, Lucian? The blood of women and men I thought were loyal to this city is on my hands this day, all because they threatened my people, and you dare speak as if I do not care for them?" She shook her head. "I did not incite the rioting! I did not drag the savants of the Temple of Ilisith from their sanctuary…." she moved her blade so that it was pointed at his heart.

"….But I will tell you what I will do, Lucian," she continued. "I will end this, here and now!"

Lucian's grin widened. "Is that a fact, Yehmina? No, no, I don't think that will do at all, I still have a great many things to do, you see, and I can't allow you or your ilk to get in my way until I've finished." He glanced past her, then, to the knot of savants.

"Now, before we were so rudely interrupted," he began, acting as if neither Yehmina nor her sword existed. "I was asking all of you a very important question...." He began walking towards the group of savants, slowly, like a predator savouring the last moments of its prey. He stopped before the first of the guards that served as a barrier between the savants and anyone who might try to intervene, his gaze passing over each one in turn before speaking his question:

"Which one of you fathered Princess Luccia?"

Many in the crowd that had gathered there gasped in astonishment. I glanced over at Luccia, but to my surprise, the princess seemed strangely thoughtful.

"I knew it," she whispered to me. "I've always known he wasn't my father. Mother nearly said as much, once. It's not that uncommon, you know? Many go to the Temple of Ilisith for assistance in such....delicate matters...." She glanced at the group of savants, suddenly concerned. "I don't think any of them will tell, though. They are under oath never to tell, as if they never sired the child in the first place."

"They could all be hurt--killed, even!" I hissed. "They have to say who it is!"

Luccia merely shrugged. "Even in the face of death, many would rather die than break their oaths made before any of the Powers, even in this day and age."

General Lucian glowered at the savants. "Well?" He snapped. "Which one of you let the Queen into your bed, hm? Which one of you played the whore for her?" His gaze passed over each one in turn.

At first, there was silence, and it seemed that Luccia was right, that the savants would be true to their oath and say nothing, and then....

"I'm the one...."

All eyes turned to the one who had spoken. It was the old man, the one who had welcomed me into the temple. He was no longer hunched over, instead standing tall and fixing General Lucian with a steely gaze.

"I fathered Princess Luccia," he stated.

"No," another man stepped from the group. "Savant Bertrand is lying. The Queen visited me that night."

"No, he's lying!" shouted another. "I'm Princess Luccia's father!"

"No, I am!"

"They're all lying, General, I'm the father!"

"They're all wrong!" A woman shouted. "I sired the princess, although it was kind of my fellows to take credit for it."

I remembered my mother saying that not all who bled were women. I supposed that if that were the case, not all who sired children were men, or third-sex, as the case may be. One by one, all of the savants replied in the affirmative, the crowd glancing back and forth between them like spectators at a debate—which, in a sense, this was—while General Lucian's scowl deepened.

Even though the situation was desperate, I couldn't help but grin. The savants wouldn't give up the name of the sire that easily. When I glanced over at Luccia, however, her expression was grim.

"Those fools," she whispered. "Damned fools, every one of them, throwing their lives away like this...."
Suddenly, General Lucian stopped scowling, and a satisfied smile spread across his face.

"Well, well," he said, taking a step closer to the savants. "I was only going to kill the one who sired that little brat, but since you have all been so forthcoming, I think I'll just save myself the headache of hunting you in the streets and kill you all where you stand," and, so saying, he made a sharp gesture towards the savants.

"Kill them all!" he cried. "And while you're at it, burn this temple to the ground; it's such an unsightly structure."

"No!" Luccia screamed, pushing her way to the very front. "Stop this at once!"

In the next moment all of the windows in the temple shattered at once. At the same time, the doors to the temple were flung open, and out came a group of savants, mostly women, but a few individuals of other genders were present, eyes all blazing with anger. I guessed that General Lucian had separated the ones who were capable of siring children with the Queen from the ones who were not, and had intended to execute the potential sires and burn the temple down with the others trapped inside.

The soldiers standing close to the door screamed as glass rained down on them, though the savants, standing in the doorway were not affected. General Lucian flung himself to the side as Grandmistress Yehmina lunged for him.

I watched, astonished, as spirits began pouring out through the open windows, and there, leading the horde of spirits, was Adebayo astride Ore, having flattened herself as she had when he had dropped me off the day he had left Kamalak's service.

"Excuse me, my siblings!" He called, landing near them. "There were a lot of soldiers, took us a while to clear them all out."

I broke free of the crowd, heedless of the attention I attracted. "Adebayo!" I called.

Adebayo turned. "Ah, hello, Hedda, or should I call you 'Princess', now?" He grinned. "Excuse me for a second, will you? Ore!"

In a matter of moments, Ore had shifted into the more human-like form that most bonded spirits adopted and promptly slammed a soldier into one of the temple's walls. There was a sickening crunch of bones, and then the would-be executioner slumped to the ground and did not move.

I stared at Ore, shocked that a spirit bonded to someone in service to Ilisith would so quickly stoop to violence. "Adebayo, i-isn't that a violation of your oath to always be in service to Love, not War?"

Adebayo shook his head. "I was the one who swore the oath, child. But Ore? Ore is perfectly free to do what she likes, as is every other spirit that resides in this temple." He glanced at General Lucian, who was currently occupied by an angry Grandmistress Yehmina. "Someone didn't consider that when he decided to assault this temple. We learned from Harok the Mad, and from Savant Chesnos, we learned not to trust all of our temple guards." He grinned at the young savant, who just now stepped from the crowd of onlookers.

"Don't tell me he's another spy?" I groaned. "Where does Ser Kainet get all these spies?"

Chesnos grinned. "Oh, I think he has a few in almost every country in the world, and a comfortably substantial network in Firehaven itself. When you're the Queen's Spymaster, a little over-preparedness can go a long way."

"How did you manage to escape, anyways?" I asked.

"Oh, that was easy," Adebayo said. "The soldiers didn't bother to check the latrines, and none of them paid much attention to the savants inside the temple. Since Harok's time, the savants have had the time to build many different passages out of the temple."

"That was how I escaped," Chesnos added. "It was a gamble, but the passage wasn't guarded."

"I stayed behind to help take care of the guards inside the temple," said Adebayo. "Speaking of which…." He paused, and then Ore slammed into another soldier who was trying to contain a treejack. "I really should get back to supporting Ore and making sure the others are well."

He gave us all a parting grin before turning back to Ore, who had thrown herself into the fray with wild abandon. Chesnos turned to where the other savants were slowly making their way out of the melee, protected by the shimmering barriers of several knight type spirits.

"I should help get everyone to safety," he remarked. "If I were you, Princess, I wouldn't stay here much longer," and with that, he ran to run alongside the knights protecting the group of savants.

He was right, of course, spirits and soldiers clashed with the temple spirits in the streets. I watched as a flamemaid collided with a metalknight and dispersed in a shower of sparks. A treemaid wrapped vines around the same metalknight and threw him into a building, and she was incinerated by another flamemaid in turn. It was a scene of complete chaos. I needed to find Luccia. I had lost sight of her when she broke free of the crowd.

Suddenly, someone grabbed my shoulder, I spun around to knock them away, but then I saw that it was Luccia, a bloody sword in her hands. "Come on!" She cried, grabbing my hand "We need to get away from here!"

"Where should we go?!" I shouted.

"Anywhere but here!"

All of a sudden I found that I couldn't see a thing as smoke clouded my vision. The general had given orders to set the temple ablaze. I could only pray that someone would be able to put the fire out in time, but I had more immediate concerns, like the safety of my sister and Leaf.

That was when General Lucian's face materialized from

out of the smoke, his mouth twisted in a sneer.

"Well, well," he purred. "I thought I heard you two before! If it isn't my dear Queen's little brat—two of her little brats, if I'm not mistaken." He held up a hand, and fire sprang from his palm.

"Well," he continued. "I suppose that since my soldiers have doubtless gutted your mother like the pig she is by now, I can at least save you the trouble of mourning her."

"Why?" I asked, hoping that I could distract him long enough to think of something. "Why are you doing this?" Lucian's face contorted into a mask of rage.

"Why?!" He cried. "She betrayed me, that loathsome little whore, cast me off like that week's refuse, when I had denied her nothing, not even the use of my own body when she asked it of me! I gave that to her willingly, but she…." The flame in his hand grew bigger with every word.

"I gave her everything." He snarled. "I gave her everything, and she repays me by jumping into that woman's bed when I had barely finished inside her!"

Somehow I knew that 'that woman' couldn't have been anyone else but my mother, and suddenly, yet more pieces of the puzzle of Firehaven fell into place.

Luccia glared the enraged general. "My mother never loved you!" She cried. "The only one who liked to pretend that that wasn't true was you, and, apparently, the soldiers you've convinced to follow you in your mad schemes!"

General Lucian's expression contorted further as Luccia finished speaking. He wasn't the man I had seen saunter up the steps the other day—arrogant but composed— now, a feral light burned in his eyes.

"I always knew you were a little brat!" He snarled. "Well, now you'll burn! You'll all burn!"

Hedda! Look out!

I yelped and jumped back as a fireball struck the ground near my feet. I had forgotten about General Lucian's flamemaid, Spark, but obviously she didn't share my oversight, and unlike the previous battle with the flamemaid, Leaf didn't have a rock to throw at her this time, and we didn't have the the advantage of surprise either. My glaive was mostly made of wood, and therefore all but useless against her.

Luccia and I began to back away as the flamemaid advanced on us, her leering master following along behind. *We have to do something, Leaf!* I sent, desperately trying to think of something.

A thought came to me, based on something that Lord Kamalak had said during one of our lessons. It was risky, but now was hardly the time for playing safe, and I needed a way to distract both the general and his flamemaid at once.

I sent the thought to Leaf, and, to my surprise, she readily agreed to it; she needed only a moment to prepare. I wished fervently that I could speak to Luccia through the bond in the same way that I could speak to Leaf, but the best I could hope for was that I would have time to grab her and run while General Lucian was distracted, provided this ploy even worked.

Leaf! Now!

In the moment it took any of us to blink, Leaf had thrown her poison darts, and Lucian and the flamemaid cried out in unison. Leaf had been aiming for the general's eye, and her aim was true.

In the next moment, I grabbed Luccia's hand.

"Run!" I screamed.

We ran, heedless of the direction in which we were going, as long as it was away from the Lion General and his fire spirit.

We turned down alleyways and ran past darkened shops and houses. No one dared leave their homes this night. I envied them their relative safety.

I turned a corner and was snatched up by someone, a hand covering my mouth before I could cry out.

"Don't scream," a voice hissed in my ear, and then I was face to face with Avna.

"What are you doing?!" I exclaimed.

Avna placed a finger over her mouth. "He wants to see you," she said.

"Hedda?" Luccia came around the corner. "What is going—" She stopped in the middle of the alley. "Who is that woman?"

"She's...." --the word 'friend' didn't seem like an appropriate term to describe Avna—"....someone we can trust," I finished, beginning to follow Avna (and Crest, who was waiting up ahead).

"But we don't have time, Hedda!" She called, running to catch up to me and Leaf. "We have to go!"

I turned around to face her. "Do you trust me, Luccia?"

"Of course I do, but—"

I shook my head. "No, no 'buts'. General Lucian won't find us. I know it sounds unbelievable, but I need you to trust me."

Luccia glanced at Avna, who was standing at the end of the alley with her customary scowl on her face, and then her gaze rested on me again. Finally, she nodded. "I trust you, Hedda."

I nodded. "Thank you for your trust," I said, taking her hand. "Let's get going...."

CHAPTER FIFTEEN

We followed Avna and Crest through the twisting alleyways. The sky was the deep blue of twilight, thousands of stars winking overhead like diamonds. It was a strangely beautiful sight, and I heard Luccia's breath catch in awe.

"How lovely," she breathed.

It was also sign that we were now in the not-place where Kamalak's Will held sway, and that was not so much comforting as it was disconcerting.

Suddenly, there were no buildings blocking my view, and we emerged into an open space where a bonfire reached to the sky. Around the bonfire, spirits and the shadowy figures of people clustered, and before it stood the god Himself, clad in armor the colour of a night with neither moon nor stars.

"Welcome, Princess Hedda, Princess Luccia, eldermaid Leaf," He said, making a far-reaching gesture that encompassed the fire and those around it. "So glad you could make it on this….auspicious….occasion…."

In the dim light, I saw Luccia's eyes narrow. "Do I know you, Ser?" She asked.

In answer, Kamalak strode up to her, grasping her chin—

causing Luccia to gasp in surprise—and tilting her head upwards to gaze into His eyes. I knew what she was seeing in those eyes; I had caught a glimpse of the dying universe behind them myself, after all, but I did not envy her this moment. "You do not know Me, Princess," He murmured. "But many of your people, the thieves and the gamblers, the liars, the poor and the desperate, they know Me, and when they call to Me, I hear them," He smiled a little, releasing her. "And sometimes, I even answer them…."

Luccia stared at Him, a look of utter astonishment on her face, the same look I had imagined I gave Him when I first gazed into those eyes, and then she fell to her knees.

"Lord Kamalak," she murmured. "But, they say the Powers are—"

"Gone?" Kamalak smiled. "No, not all of Us abandoned this world and its mortals to their own folly, though not all mortals realize it." He turned to me, then, and this time his smile had lost its knife edge. "And how is one of My Champions, My Hedda?" He asked.

"I don't feel like anyone's Champion," I grumbled.

"Well, I should not think so, for you have not been in any great battles yet," He remarked, sparing a glance for Luccia, who was still kneeling among the cobblestones, and gesturing for her to rise. "You might as well get up," He told her. "There's no sense in ruining perfectly good cobblestones."

Luccia rose slowly and began to brush the stones and dirt from her riding clothes. "What do You mean, when You said that Hedda is Your Champion?"

"I mean what I said, girl!" Kamalak snapped, causing Luccia to flinch. "What do your fool tutors teach you at court, besides how to be a pretty little puppet?"

Luccia glared at the god, and I had to admire her courage.

"I am not a puppet, Lord Kamalak," she stated, drawing herself up to her full height, and in that moment, she looked the very picture of a young Queen-to-Be. "I am my mother's daughter, my mother, who is Beloved of Menaishe, Beloved of Your Father Ilisith, Queen Sofiya the First, and I will not hide here while my people are in danger!"

Silence descended on the scene, and for a moment, I swore that even the bonfire was silent, the fire spirits playing within pausing at their sport. All eyes turned towards the Son of Ilisith.

Kamalak began to clap slowly, His smile holding the barest hint of warmth for the young princess.

"Good, very good," He murmured. "Well, very good, for a noble, which admittedly is not saying much…you might make a fine Queen yet.…" He took a step back from her, shifting to include Leaf and I in the conversation, Avna and Crest had moved to a comfortable spot close to the bonfire, though, like Leaf, Crest was at the farthest point away from the deadly flames.

"Now," Kamalak continued. "It remains to be seen whether you can manage to not get yourselves killed this night. General Lucian is *hot on your heels*…"—and here He chuckled at His own joke—"…at the moment."

He turned and walked back to the bonfire, the earth and stone springing up to form a chair for Him, and there He sat, stroking His chin thoughtfully.

"So now there is a question you must ask yourselves.…" He began, leaning forward in His chair, "…..and that is what do you intend to do when your time with Me is at an end?"

"Actually.…" I began. "….I—we—were sort of hoping You could tell us what we should do.…"

Kamalak gave me his cat-smile. "My dear girl," He

164

purred. "If I told you that, it would hardly be fair to your opponent...."

"Lord, if You will forgive my saying so," Luccia interjected. "I would not expect that the God of Thieves would play fair in much of anything, much less life."

"True," Kamalak conceded. "But sometimes 'tis interesting to see how the game plays out when one has finished arranging all the pieces to one's liking, and I rather think I would enjoy watching this game play out on its own." His chair sank back into the ground as He rose and turned to face the fire, and I watched as the shadowy figures of His not-quite-savants dispersed, intent on whatever tasks He had set for them this night. I wondered how many He had lost in the riots at the Old City.

"One is too many," He said suddenly, as if I had spoken the words out loud. "Yemena has already gathered them to Her Bosom, I have already chosen some to attend Me in My Court. The others were claimed by other Powers, or are to be reborn." He gazed into the fire, and it seemed as if it would be a sacrilege to destroy the sense of solemnity that hung over us with mere words.

Luccia bit her lip. "It may not mean much to You, Lord Kamalak, but I am sorry for all the lives this city has lost this day, and for the destruction of the dwellings within." Kamalak half turned to regard her, one eye shining in the dark. "Do not mourn for those who are lost, mortal. The tears of the living are of no use to the dead."

"Still," Luccia pressed on, her expression resolute, "one of us has done much to offend You. I would make amends, if I could, or perhaps my mother—"

"--My Champions will avenge the fallen," Kamalak interrupted. "As for reparations, should you survive, we will have much to discuss, then again…." He smirked. "Should either you or your mother die, mayhap I will simply extract the blood-payment from your shades."

This gave Luccia pause. "My mother is alive?"

"Did I say that?" Kamalak queried innocently. "Well, I suppose you were going to find that out sooner or later." He made a familiar dismissive gesture with one hand. "Now, I believe you have something important to do. Go now, and in the Holy Names of all the Powers, try to survive." His dismissive gesture abruptly changed to one of benediction.

"Good Luck, children!" He called, and His smile once again had that knife edge to it. "Do try to avoid being roasted alive! I have spent much of My time preparing you for this, Hedda, and 'twould be a shame to be forced to find someone else to take your place due to your untimely demise."

And then, without any warning, the bonfire disappeared, and we were back where we had started as if our meeting with the god had never happened, and the crackling sound that reached my ears was not a human-made fire, but a flamemaid, Spark, and where Spark was, the man chasing us could not be far behind.

"We have to run! Luccia hissed, grabbing my hand. "There has to be a safe place somewhere in this city!"
I shook my head. "I don't think there is!" I whispered back. "He'll just keep hunting us—and anyone else who opposes him—until he gets what he wants."

"We can't just give up, Hedda!" Leaf chimed in. "Flamemaid or no flamemaid, I'll destroy that man if he so much as singes a hair on your head!"

I heard footsteps approaching us, and then General Lucian's voice rang out.

"Children, children!" He called. "Where did you go, my

dear, sweet princesses?"

"Hide!" I hissed, and pressed my back against the wall as Leaf changed into an elderberry and stowed herself away in one of my pockets.

"I don't see them anywhere," said a female voice that I assumed belonged to Spark.

"Just....keep....looking!" Lucian snarled. "That little bitch will pay for what she did to my eye!"

I glanced over at Luccia, who was opposite me in the alley. She gestured that we should proceed down it. Slowly, we inched away from the sound of General Lucian's voice, I uttering a quick prayer to Lord Kamalak, Son of Ilisith to hide us in the shadows. It felt so strange, praying to a deity with Whom I had just conversed not a moment before.

Then, something that was nothing short of miraculous happened.

As I watched, the shadows in the alley seemed to move to cover us, and I heard a voice whisper in my head the way Leaf did. *Go,* they said. *We shall guard your escape.*
Spirits, I thought. *They have to be some sort of spirit.* But I had no time to think on it, for Luccia was tugging on my arm, leading me away. The shadows were pouring out of the alley like a river of ink, but they felt more like the honour guards that escorted royalty during important functions.

When we reached the end of the alley, the shadows didn't seem to completely disperse, rather, two of them detached from the whole and began moving up the street.

Follow, came the whispers.

"Do you hear that voice?" Luccia whispered to me. "It....doesn't sound like it's coming from anywhere, and yet, I hear it."

I nodded. "We call it sending, it's the way spirits

communicate with humans."

"Then the shadows….the shadows are spirits?" She asked.

"I don't know," I admitted. "I think they could be. I just thought of asking Lord Kamalak for help."

"I thought He said He wanted to see how the game played out," Luccia remarked.

I shrugged. "He is a god, who knows what He considers to be 'letting the game play out'?"

Luccia nodded. "My mother told me stories of the God of Thieves, but I had always imagined that he had left with the other Powers. I suppose the world is always in need of Luck, though."

"The world is always in need of the things the other Powers gave us, as well," I replied. "I suppose that is why They created the spirits, but perhaps there are no spirits that best embody Luck, save Kamalak Himself."

"Perhaps we should leave such things to the savants to puzzle over," Luccia mused. "Where are the shadows leading us, anyways?"

I glanced around, trying to find my bearings, but as with the first time I had met with Kamalak, it seemed as if all the buildings were identical, and for a moment I cursed myself for not taking the time to explore the city.

Luccia suddenly stopped. "I think I know this place," she said, glancing around. "I think—I think I know where the shadows are leading us."

"Well, wherever they're leading us," I remarked. "I only hope it's not into a trap."

"And on that, we agree," said Luccia.

CHAPTER SIXTEEN

The shadows led us to Spirits' Park. Its official name was Kinarshe's Eye, but everyone called it by its other name because of the unusual quantity of non-bonded spirits that made their home in the natural setting. It was a popular destination for those seeking to bond with a spirit who did not intend to travel far from the city. Not everyone who came to the park had that wish granted, of course. Many simply came to enjoy the scenery and the park's famous fountain, one of the few human-made structures in the place.

"I thought they would bring us here," Luccia remarked as she gazed up at the fountain, watching the sprays of water as the watermaids that lived in the fountain frolicked, heedless of any danger, or really, heedless of anything that wasn't another watermaid. Once again, I found myself envying another's good fortune that night.

The shadows had dispersed throughout the park, but now one rose up and came towards us, or, more accurately, towards Luccia.

"The heretic nears," said the shadow spirit, a distinctively masculine tone to his voice leading me to conclude that he was possibly a knight type, if, indeed, these were spirits Kamalak had summoned, and not constructs like the shadow woman I had fought during my training sessions.

Luccia turned to me. "We can't keep running," she stated.

"I know," I agreed. "But what choice do we have? We can't possibly win against him in a fight…"

You can, Hedda, Leaf sent. *Lord Kamalak Himself taught you how to fight, after all!*

It's not that simple, I sent back, aloud, I said "As long as he has Spark with him, none of us stand a chance."

One of the shadow spirits took a step towards Luccia. "You have not yet bonded," xe stated.

"No," she replied, looking to me as if for confirmation that she was saying the right thing. "The royal family traditionally does not bond with spirits, it's—"

"—I would bond with you," said the spirit.

"….Tradition…." Luccia finished, and then she seemed to realize what the spirit had actually said. "P-Pardon me?"

"I would bond with you," xe repeated.

"But, it's not—"

Something occurred to me then. "Luccia," I said. "My mother is bonded as well, and I have Leaf. There's no reason you can't still be Queen while spirit-bonded, the spirits are always the ones who do the choosing, after all."

There was a long pause before Luccia responded. "You're

right," she said, nodding as she turned to the spirit. "I will bond with you," she told xir, "and face my mother when no one's actively trying to kill me." She glanced at me. "How do we--?"

I hesitated. "Normally you….take a bit of the spirit into yourself," I explained. "But—"I glanced at the spirit. "I'm not sure…."

But the spirit seemed to know what to do, as I watched, xe seemed to sink down into the ground, stretching out from Luccia's feet like a living shadow. *Xe is her shadow!* I realized, watching the dark shape resolve into a slightly bulkier but still humanoid shape.

"I am Umbra," xe said. "I shall follow you."

Luccia gasped, turning to me, astonished. "So, this is what it feels like…."

I nodded. "You might feel a little discomfort at first, though," I warned. "It was like that for me when I bonded with Leaf."

Luccia was silent for a moment. "I don't feel anything like that," she said. "Xir thoughts are very….quick….almost jumbled." She shook her head as if trying to clear it.

"Quick and jumbled? Somehow, that seems appropriate for a jack type spirit…."

"—I thought I heard someone near the fountain," that voice, belonging to General Lucian's flamemaid, Spark, was a stark reminder that we were both still in peril.

Luccia grabbed my arm. "Umbra!" She hissed. "Can you hide both of us? Like you did before?"

The shadowjack must have sent back a reply in the affirmative, for xe rose up, covering both of us in a cloak of deepest darkness.

Jack types are adept at creating illusions, but this did not feel like a mere illusion.

It was none too soon, for Spark came into view a moment later, her touch scorching the grass around her as she went ahead of General Lucian. By the light created by her corona, I could see that the general's right eye was dark and swollen, no doubt due to the dart that Leaf had thrown.

"Are you certain they went this way?" He snarled.

"The Palace is ours," Spark replied. "They came in this direction, of that I am certain, or your soldiers would have found them by now."

"Few of my soldiers are left now, thanks to that bitch Yehmina," Lucian growled as he neared the fountain. "Children? Where are you, my dears?"

"I see no place where they could be hiding," Spark said as she neared the fountain.

Lucian scowled. "Burn it to the ground!" He spat. "That will flush them out, that's what I should have told the soldiers I sent out for their mother this afternoon."

For the first time that I had seen, the expression on Spark's face was something other than carefully neutral.

"But—the Custom!" She stammered, horrified. Even bonded spirits were hesitant to come so close to breaking the Custom of not harming their wild brethren.

"I care not for your Custom!" Lucian roared, so close that I feared he would see me flinch and know that we were hiding there. "Burn it to the ground! Burn it all!"

For a moment, I thought that Spark was going to argue with him. It wouldn't have been the first time a spirit had actively worked against her bondmate, but then she sighed and raised her arms, fire racing down her body as she prepared to unleash her power.

I had to do something, and at that moment, I could only

think of one thing to do. *Leaf! The fountain!* I screamed in my head.

Umbra and Leaf were already moving, however, and, as I watched, the shadow that was covering me slid away, and the two spirits—Leaf had found a rock to help guard against the flames--had pushed Spark into the fountain. The watermaids, sensing an intrusion into their realm, quickly swarmed the fallen flamemaid.

And then, there was nothing left of Spark but steam that rose from the fountain like incense.

Lucian bellowed in rage and pain, falling to his knees and clutching his head as if an angry creature was trying to break out of it. When he looked up at me, his face was contorted with rage, and then, without warning he lunged at me.

"You….you….you!" He howled as he slashed at me with his sword.

"Would have given you everything….yes….everything!" He howled. "….But now you have taken my Spark….yes….took her away….so now I'm going to take you away, you, and your city!"

I jumped back; reaching back to draw my glaive, but Luccia was the one who closed the gap between us, sword raised like an avenging goddess, like Menaishe Herself. "No! No you won't!" She screamed, slashing at the enraged general.

"Ungrateful child!" Lucian spat as the two of them separated, bodies taut as they focused on the other. "You forget….who raised you…."

"I remember perfectly well who raised me," Luccia replied. "My mother was always there for me, but you, you never cared!"

"Oh, why would I care for a savant's brat?!" He spat, and

then, for the barest of moments, his gaze locked on mine. "But you," he said. "Yes, you, I would have….but she took you away…."

I pointed the tip of the glaive at him, once again, that familiar chill running up my spine. "What are you talking about?"

He smiled. "Got you off her, I did, but then she took you away….far away….were you living with that little bitch of hers?" His expression changed to one that was almost gleeful. "And then….then she said she would take me back, but I knew, oh yes….I knew where she'd been lying…."

I nearly fell over in shock. *My father?! This man claims to be my father!?* But I kept the tip of the glaive leveled at his throat. "I don't have a father," I said. "I have two mothers, and even if I did have a father, he wouldn't be a monster like you!"

General Lucian laughed; the high-pitched peals of a man who had truly lost all sense.

"Well, I suppose it doesn't matter anyways!" He sneered. "It doesn't change the fact that I am going to kill you, my dear….sweet….*daughter!*"

He lunged for me again, but this time I was ready, blocking his blow with the flat end of my blade, and using the shaft to keep some distance between us. He spun away from me abruptly to engage Luccia and Leaf in turn, like a furious storm wind, and I had to admire his skill in being able to handle groups of opponents, especially while debilitated by the loss of his spirit and blind in one eye, to say nothing of the injuries he had sustained in the battle with Grandmistress Yehmina. What had happened to her at the Temple of Ilisith? I didn't remember seeing her fall.

It was past time for thinking, however, I did not think as I fought with Luccia, Leaf, and Umbra against General Lucian, I simply moved, the way Kamalak had taught me.

And then I heard Leaf scream, and a blinding pain in my arm caused me to lose my balance and stumble backwards. Seeing his chance, Lucian bore down on me…..
….Suddenly, my dagger was in my hand, sliding through the cracks in his armor….
….I heard a gasp, and then I realized that it had not come from my mouth, but his….

--And then Leaf drove her spear-branches into his throat.

CHAPTER SEVENTEEN

I opened my eyes to the deep blue of early evening. *No, this isn't right,* I thought as I sat up. Well, for one thing, there was no weight on my chest. What had happened? I remembered stabbing General Lucian—*my father*—and then…. *Then I had awakened here….*

But where was here? I glanced around. The sky was a deep blue dotted with millions of blinking lights and strange swirling patterns, like delicate lace on a ball gown. I glanced down at my feet, and saw that I rested on verdant grass. Had I somehow been moved away from the fountain?

"No, My Child, you are in My realm, now…."

I jumped to my feet, startled, and turned towards the voice.

"Who are you?" I called. "Where am I?"

As I watched, the night sky seemed to shift before me, like fabric—no, it actually *was* fabric—a cloak fashioned of the sky and stars themselves. The woman wearing the cloak had hair the color of black obsidian and lips as red as ripe apples. Her skin was ashen and her eyes were the same teardrop shape of Grandmistress Yehmina's eyes.

And she was smiling, a smile like the sunrise, a smile like that of a nurturing mother for her children, a smile that was kind and somehow….infinite.

As quickly as I had risen, I fell to my knees. Of all the Powers, it is said, Four left, but One remained.

"Lady Yemena," I murmured.

The Goddess of Death's smile broadened. "Indeed, Child," She said. "I have been collecting a few more souls than usual in Firehaven tonight, but there is one last soul I need to take."

I swallowed nervously, and found I had no saliva left to swallow.

"Mine?" I asked in a small voice.

"Ah, no," She said. "You were not grievously wounded in the battle." She drew back Her cloak, and I saw that She held the prone form of General Lucian close to Her.

"I was simply wondering," said the Goddess of Death. "If you wished to say anything more to your father before I send him on his way."

For a moment, I thought that I should say something about how I imagined that he would have been a good man, if I had only known him, or if my mothers had made different choices, but then I turned away.

None of this was the fault of my mother—neither of them.

"I have nothing more to say to him," I said, decisively.

Yemena's smile never wavered. "As you wish," She said. "He does not deserve your forgiveness, but the wounds that you bear from this battle will take that much longer to heal as a result, all actions have their consequences."

She gave the man in Her arms a pointed glance. "In the end, all debts are paid."

"W-What will happen to him?" I asked, suddenly curious.

"He will be given to Kamalak, for a time," the goddess replied, "and then I shall take him to My bosom, where many of the dead rest, and perhaps, someday, he will have the chance to live a better life."

I shuddered at the thought of what Lord Kamalak would do to him, though I knew it was just. There was something else I wanted to ask Her, though, before I returned to waking consciousness.

"I, Lady—" I began. "The other Powers, do They—are They real? Do They still watch over us, even a little?" Yemena's eternal smile broadened. "My dear Child, you already know the answer to that question. You have always known the answer," and with that, She drew her cloak of stars over General Lucian. Stars burst behind my eyes and I knew no more.

Luccia told me what happened afterwards, how I had passed out from the shock, and she and Umbra worked to pull the body off of me. My mother and the Queen finally arrived, bringing with them a full contingent of the Order of Menaishe and a very irate Grandmistress Yehmina. Grandmistress Yehmina, it turned out, had lost track of him when the fire in the temple had started, although she had managed to strike a blow that had eventually weakened him enough so that Leaf and I could finish him off. I told no one how, even weakened, he had almost succeeded in murdering us.

General Lucian's body was taken and buried without ceremony, with not even a marker to indicate his final resting place. Luccia told me that Ember wished to burn it, but mother had stayed her hand, saying that it wouldn't have been appropriate for a traitor to be given a great hero's sendoff, and the Queen agreed with her.

I awoke in the Temple of Kinarshe. At least, I imagined it was the temple, because looming over me was Flower. The cherryjack nodded to xirself as my eyes flooded open.

"Ah, good," xe said. "I had the utmost confidence in my abilities, of course, but still, it is a relief to see that you have awakened at last." Xe turned xir head, and then the door burst open and Leaf, Ember, and Umbra crowded into the room. "You're awake!" Leaf exclaimed. "Well, I knew—because of the bond, but *Ser* Flower would not let us into the room." "You would only have smothered her!" Flower snapped. "I require no distractions while I work." Xe drew back from my bedside. "Kindly do not cause her stress, eldermaid, she is still mending."

Leaf watched Flower go before turning to me. "You should have seen xir earlier, Hedda!" She said. "Xe had drawn on the energy of all the other tree spirits in the temple to conjure up a hedge around it, came close to killing us all as we approached the temple."

"Yes," Queen Sofiya nudged Leaf aside. "That's why I'm introducing a motion to make the 'Ser' official, Flower deserves as much, and more. How are you, my dear?"

"Well….I can see…." I remarked, attempting to sit up and feeling my entire body ache in protest. "But I feel as if I've just run into a knight's shield."

Queen Sofiya nodded. "You sustained quite a wound, it was lucky Luccia was there to staunch the bleeding." She frowned. "I still don't know how I feel about the bond she formed," she said, glancing at Umbra, "but if the information she has given me is correct, I owe xir a great debt."

"Will you tell me....Luccia and I...." I amended. "Will you finally tell us the whole story?"

"Yes," she replied, nodding solemnly. "But tomorrow, I think. You need to rest.

"I...know...." I replied, suddenly inexplicably drowsy.

"Rest well, child," said the Queen--my mother.

CHAPTER EIGHTEEN

The next day, a full contingent of members of the Order of Menaishe, led by Grandmistress Yehmina herself—none the worse for wear despite her ordeal—came to the Temple of Kinarshe to escort Leaf, mother, Ember and I to the Palace. Flower gave them quite the scare when xe nearly raised the hedge around the temple again, but was quickly calmed when sie learned that xe was to be made a knight that afternoon. "I still do not trust these soldiers," xe informed us as xe walked with us alongside xir bondmate, the Head of the Order of Kinarshe, who was blind.

Grandmistress Yehmina scowled at the treejack, but xir bondmate held up a hand. "Peace, Yehmina," xe said. "It has been a trying time for all of us, these last few days, and your Order did not even take the brunt of the abuse." Yehmina's scowl deepened, and the Head of the Order smiled.

It occurred to me that xe was probably using the bond between xirself and xir treejack to see, or perhaps Flower was describing what was happening through the bond.

"You had better both behave yourselves when you go before the Queen, both of you," Yehmina grumbled, and I thought I heard the barest hint of affection for the Head of the Order in her voice.

The Head and Flower wore matching grins as the Head said "Of course, Yehmina," at which point the Grandmistress merely sighed and turned her attention to the road again.

We arrived at the Palace and were quickly ushered into the throne room. Besides the Queen, the Princess (both dressed in full regalia of white and gold) and Umbra, there were a great many people there, noble and commoner alike, but despite the size of the crowd, the atmosphere was remarkably subdued. Even more surprising, though, was the way in which we were announced, Princess Hedda I expected, though it was still strange to hear the title applied thus, but I was certainly not expecting them to announce my mother as *General* Augusta. Was this a sign that she was replacing General Lucian, or had she held the position before her exile?

When we all made obeisance before the throne, the Queen held up a hand for silence, which rapidly descended on the already near-noiseless crowd.

"Much has happened in the past few days," she began. "General Augusta, whom you had thought banished from my presence and exiled, had returned, and some of you began to wonder whether I would enforce her exile." She raised her head. "I shall tell you truly this day: Lady—General— Augusta's exile was a lie from the very start!"

I heard no gasps of surprise, but there was a general murmur among the crowd. I wondered if it had not been known already, that this was perhaps, merely a formality, and official gesture by the Queen before her Court.

Queen Sofiya bowed her head. "You all knew of my relationship with General Augusta," she stated. "What you did not know, however, was that we had decided to have a child together," and here she glanced at me, and I suddenly felt the weight of hundreds of eyes on me. I wanted nothing more to hide from those gazes. Leaf, sensing my thoughts, moved closer to me, even Flower shifted a little to conceal me from their eyes.

"As many of you well know," the Queen continued. "The Temple of Ilisith makes certain…provisions….for those unable to have children to be given that opportunity," she sighed, and I watched her shoulders slump. "At that time, there was a man in this Court who was rapidly rising through the ranks of the Order of Menaishe. He was a good friend of mine, so I suggested…." and here she raised her head, and I thought I glimpsed tears glistening in her eyes.

"I suggested that he should be our child's sire, that I would invite him to share my bed, for Augusta has only ever been attracted to women," her voice cracked, and she glanced at my mother. "Augusta, I should have listened to you!"

Mother shook her head. "No, I agreed to it as well, it would hardly have made any difference."
The Queen gave a little shake of her head before continuing. "The result of that union is the young woman who comes before you today," she said. "Princess Hedda, whom I acknowledge as my daughter before the Court and all the Powers, but that is not the end of the tale…." She glanced at Luccia, reaching over to grasp her hand. "Lucian had always been envious of Augusta, I think he imagined that I would put her aside once Hedda was born, but it was quite the opposite. I

knew he plotted against us, and so I sent Augusta away with the child, making it seem that they were exiled, when in fact, her standing in this court had not changed, but only a few knew this to be true."

Kainet was one of the people closest to the throne, and I thought I saw him smile at that, though Seed was as impassive as ever.

"But you, my people, made it clear that you desired an heir," she continued, and I saw her gaze pointedly at a cluster of nobles near the front, who began to glance at each other nervously. "I could not bear Lucian's touch any longer, not even for you, and so I went to the Temple of Ilisith, and the realm was blessed by the birth of Princess Luccia."
She drew herself up in her throne, and she was no longer the mother who had sent away her daughter, nor the woman who felt the weight of her past deeds settle on her shoulders, but the Queen, protector of her people.

"That is the truth of it!" She cried. "That is the secret I and Augusta have borne all these years, and the events of the last few days was the price we paid for keeping that secret!" Her hands were white with tension as she gripped the armrests of her throne, but suddenly, they went slack.

"Today, we make amends," she said, a grim finality in her voice. "Today, we mourn the dead. We cleanse the streets that have been poisoned by violence, and we move forward, always forward!" She glanced at my mother, and the smile was as bright as the sun. She rose from the throne, offering my mother her hand. "Augusta?"

"Yes, Your Majesty?"

"Let's start over," she said. "Will you be my Consort?"

"You don't have to ask, Your Majesty," said mother, smiling. "The answer was, is, and will always be yes."

The sound of cheering was deafening, only intensifying as the Queen crushed Augusta's lips to hers. "I have been waiting forever to give you that kiss," I heard her murmur.

"Mmm, I will pray for many more kisses, then," mother murmured.

All of a sudden, the cheering ceased, and the only sound in the room was the sound of hands slowly clapping, and all heads turned to see from where the sound originated.

"Nicely done, Your Majesty," said Kamalak. "Or should I say 'Your Majesties', yes, you will be married soon, after all." He strode down the aisle, shadow spirits following at His feet like faithful hounds, and as He passed by, those assembled there, nobles, commoners, and spirits alike, fell to their knees. My mothers faced the god, hands knitted together.

"Lord Kamalak, Son of Ilisith, I presume?" said the Queen as she descended the steps of the dais, ivory skirts rippling like water as she too, knelt before the god.

"Indeed," Kamalak replied, smiling that knife-smile. "There is a trifling matter that we must discuss, and I am afraid it cannot wait."

"Surely this matter must be of some import if one of the Powers has deigned to grace us with Their august presence?" she replied.

"Just so," said the God of Thieves. "The matter I speak of is one of justice….of reparation….for My people who were killed in the Old City, and in the years before that, when you allowed that jealous general of yours to spill the blood of My Own in the streets."

At this, the Queen bowed her head, as a condemned criminal before the executioner. "Name Your price," she murmured.

The Son of Ilisith opened His mouth to speak, but then

Luccia sprang to her feet.

"Lord!" She cried. "Your Father even offered mercy to King Harok, whom everyone knew bore the full brunt of the guilt for his crimes, would You extend that mercy to one who allowed such to happen, but did not wield the blade herself?" Kamalak glared at Luccia, who sank down to her knees again. "I was hardly intending to kill her, child!" He snapped. "The few that died and belonged to Me are with Me now, as is the one who murdered them, for a time, at least." He glanced down at Sofiya. "Killing you would accomplish little and complicate much. No, I have far more....constructive....ways that you may be put to use...." So saying, he pulled the Queen to her feet.

"Now," He said. "This is what I desire of you...."

EPILOGUE

A new temple stands in the Old City now.

It is a small, unassuming building, lit softly by candlelight, and within, a statue of the God of Thieves-- his hand raised in benediction, and smiling his knife-edged smile--stands surrounded by offerings of sweets and coin. Adjacent to the temple, workers are busy building a gigantic complex to house some of the Old City's most poverty-stricken citizens. All nobles are required to aid in its construction, which is closely monitored by shadow spirits to make sure none of them shirk their duties. Not even the royal family is exempt, the Queen herself helping to lay the foundation in the same dirty smock as everyone else. Earlier that day, the Queen was stripped of her garments and paraded naked to the Temple of Ilisith, where she made an offering to Ilisith the Sadist, who is also known as the Parent of Luck, because He was both Father and Mother to Lord Kamalak.

That evening, a wedding is celebrated, the marriage of a Queen and her new Queen-Consort, and all are invited to join in the celebrations. One spirit is knighted; xe made xir own armor from cherry wood, and stood watch over it all night in the Temple of Kinarshe, because xe did not trust that the flames in the Temple of Menaishe would stay in their sconces. Two princesses swear before Ilisith the Ruler of Love, Who blesses friendships, that they will always be joined in sisterhood. The Queen passes sweeping reforms, granting the common folk many seats on her Council, and working with Grandmistress Yehmina to institute tougher restrictions on guards and harsher penalties for guards who abuse their power. A great many criminals—some whose only crime was to be in the wrong place at the wrong time, are granted full pardons, including a certain ex-pirate named Avna. The winds of change are blowing steadily. All is well in the City of Firehaven.

And then, one day, Queen-Consort Augusta turns to her daughter, Princess Hedda, and says "I never did take you to Seacliff, did I?"

And I laugh, and say. "No, mother, you never did!"

"Ah, well," she says, tousling my hair, even though I am a grown woman and too old for such things. "I suppose that will be an adventure for another day."

"So long as the whole family gets to come," I say. "You, me, Leaf, Umbra, and the Queen—er—mother, too."
My mother snakes an arm around my waist, holding me close to her side.

"Always," she says, grinning.

"Always."

EXTRAS

THE GENESIS OF HOUSE HILLUCK: A TALE OF THE DISTANT PAST

Once, during the time when the Powers still walked the land, in the years before They withdrew from the world, there was a small village nestled at the foot of a hill near Firehaven. It was a sleepy village where nothing much happened. It was the sort of village nobles would visit to get away from their lives in the city (and, indeed, the village profited handsomely from such tourists). As it was a haven for all those seeking peace and quiet, so the village was named, and Haven Hill sheltered it like a mother sheltering a child.

As of late, however; Haven had been afflicted with Troubles.

The first of these Troubles was discovered by a widow, a short dark-skinned woman named Constance Dasherell, when she went to milk her sole cow, Kina, early one morning in early spring. That morning, she arrived at the barn only to discover—much to her bewilderment—that someone had swapped Kina's head with her tail!

Concerned for Kina's wellbeing, for she had never before encountered a cow with a head where its hindquarters should be, Ms. Dasherell made her way immediately to see the mayor, who, as it turns out, was inundated with complaints from residents and guests of the town. Guests at the inn complained that the water they were bathing or washing in kept changing temperature. The blacksmith claimed that xir finished swords had inexplicably dulled blades. The local baker claimed that her bread did not rise, and, in what was surely the most heinous of the Troubles in the town; the local bookseller claimed that someone had written in the margins and made crude doodles in all of his books, even the ones kept under lock and key.

The mayor, who, it must be said, had had little chance to rest since the Troubles began, immediately called a town meeting to discuss what could be done. The townspeople discussed the Troubles long into the night. Some were eager to blame the Troubles on the young, or the tourists, or the weather. Others were sure that it was a mischievous spirit, and casting furtive glances at the bonded among them. The mayor listened patiently to every argument and opinion on the matter and at last announced that xe would dispatch a messenger to the temple of Sudrask to ask for their assistance in investigating the matter. Many of the townspeople were satisfied by the ruling, though some left the meeting grumbling that they could not tolerate the Troubles for one moment longer. Even so, knowing they could do little about it 'til morning, the residents of the town of Haven retired to their beds.

It was a day or two after the messenger had been sent that she returned with a savant of Sudrask, who spent an entire week investigating the town and its Troubles, questioning the residents and investigating homes and businesses that were afflicted with the most troublesome Troubles. The savant quickly concluded that a Rogue was the one responsible for the Troubles, and xe had made xir home on Haven Hill. She advised the townspeople to leave food and drink to placate the troublesome spirit. The townspeople followed the savant's instructions with gusto, leaving food and drink at the foot of Haven Hill and petitioning the spirit to cease the Troubles. The mayor even offered a reward to anyone who could rid the town of the Troubles. Alas, despite their best efforts, the Troubles did not cease, in fact, the Troubles in the town seemed to increase. Many believed that the savant had not been thorough enough in her investigation. Others frustrated by the Troubles, wanted to burn Haven Hill to the ground, and still others maintained that there was no Rogue of Haven Hill, and the Troubles had some other cause.

A full month after the visit from the savant of the Order of Sudrask, a visitor arrived in town, dragging a cart laden with weapons and scraps of metal behind xir. Instead of stopping at an inn, which would have been expected of a traveler, however; the strange individual made for the town hall and asked to meet with the mayor right away.

The mayor was certainly not expecting such a request, but agreed to see the stranger anyways. The stranger introduced xirself as a blacksmith by trade who was on xir way to open a shop in Firehaven. Word had reached the surrounding towns of Haven's troubles and its cause, xe said, but xe thought xe had a solution, and had elected to approach the mayor first for permission to ascend Haven Hill.

Now, the mayor was by nature a skeptical person, and could not quite believe that a blacksmith could succeed where many others had failed, but xe was willing to try anything, as far too many families had already moved out of the town due to the Troubles. The blacksmith thanked the mayor for xir trust and promised to head out to Haven Hill in the morning.

The next morning, the blacksmith went with xir cart to Haven Hill. At the foot of the hill, xe paused and, with the confused townsfolk watching, began to dig a hole at its base. When xe was satisfied with the size of the hole (which was quite large), xe placed the shovel in its place in the cart and began to haul it up the hill.

When xe made it to the very top of the hill, the blacksmith sat on the hard ground next to it and began eating a sandwich xe had brought for the midday meal. When xe had finished eating, xe brushed the crumbs from xir trousers and stood, and then xe began to wail and cry and make such a noise that it disturbed the birds nearby.

Soon enough, the Rogue appeared, summoned by the blacksmith's keening. Xe was golden-eyed and gray-fleshed like a mountain, and although xe was at least as tall as five blacksmiths stacked atop one another, the blacksmith was not afraid, and continued sniffling in a pathetic manner.

"Why do you cry, traveler? Hush! It is annoying, and I am not in the best mood today!" The Rogue cried. The blacksmith sniffed. "What has annoyed you so, ser?" "I delighted in tricking the residents of this town," the Rogue replied. "But lately it has grown dull, the humans so predictable."

The blacksmith knew then that this was the Rogue of Haven Hill that xe sought.

"Alas, we are two of a kind!" The blacksmith exclaimed. "For I came to find the gold beneath Haven Hill, and now I have no tools with which to dig!" Hearing this, the Rogue was very much interested in the gold, and demanded to know what the blacksmith had heard of it. Through xir tears, the blacksmith told the Rogue of a great treasure that a noble buried under Haven Hill, then died before she could tell anyone where she had hidden it. "I am the heir to this treasure," xe finished sadly. "But see," and here xe pointed to the hole xe had dug at the foot of the hill, then gestured to the cart with all its broken tools. "I have already worn out all my tools from searching for it."

Now, this Rogue was quite greedy, and upon hearing this, thought to xirself: "I will trick the blacksmith and take the gold for myself!" Oh, the tricks xe could play with such gold! So xe smiled and made a great show of being magnanimous, saying: "I shall help you find the gold, good ser, for I know this hill as well as I know myself." Hearing this, the blacksmith was elated, and thanked the Rogue profusely.

The Rogue began to dig, throwing up great clods of dirt and making a terrible racket, but the blacksmith was unafraid, seating xirself atop xir cart to watch.

By the time the Rogue of Haven Hill had completed a full day's worth of digging—a job that would have taken a group of humans at least a month—Haven Hill was little more than a pit, and as the Rogue frantically searched for the treasure, the blacksmith could not help but smile to xirself.

"What is so amusing?" the Rogue demanded from the bottom of the pit.

"I was just thinking of how absurd it is that anyone would believe that a noble would ever make such an effort to hide a treasure," xe replied. "Nobles are unaccustomed to hard work, after all."

Upon hearing this, and realizing xe had been tricked, and there was no treasure to be found, the Rogue began to laugh, and xir laughter shook the ground so much so that the townspeople were concerned it would destroy the town.

"Oh, that was a grand trick!" The Rogue exclaimed, climbing out of the pit xe had worked so hard to dig. "A grand trick indeed!" And xe was so impressed with the blacksmith's cleverness that xe vowed never to harass the town of Haven again and blessed the blacksmith in the name of the God of Luck, who delights in trickery, that xe might never have an unlucky day.

And so, the Troubles ceased, and the Town of Haven became prosperous once more. The grateful mayor gave the blacksmith xir promised purse of gold. Eventually, the tale spread, and word reached distant shores of a blacksmith who had bested the Rogue of Haven Hill. It was said of this blacksmith that ever since that event, xe had never once lost a game of cards, and had even beaten the God of Luck Himself.

As for the blacksmith xirself, xe opened a shop in Firehaven, which became so popular that nobles and even the king at the time competed for the best pieces, because of xir service to the king, the blacksmith was given a title and a great mansion, and xe was happy and prosperous all the days of xir life.

To this day, the heirs of House Hilluck are said to be blessed by the God of Luck, and, as for the Rogue of Haven Hill, xe has been silent since that time. Perhaps xe is still trying to think of a better trick than the one that was played on xir all those years ago.

GUIDE TO THE POWERS

THE FIVE

Menaishe – Lady of War
Ilisith – Lord of Love
Kinarshe – Ruler of Nature
Sudrask – Lord of Knowledge
Yemena – Lady of Death

THE LESSER POWERS

Kamalak – Lord of Luck

THE SPIRITS

The spirits are sometimes known as the lesser powers. Spirits may be wild (non-bonded), bonded (to a person) or land-bonded and can be grouped into three base categories.

Maids are feminine spirits. They are known for being highly aggressive and territorial, of all spirits, maids have the most control over elemental forces. Maids generally bond with women in particular or feminine people in general. Land-bonded maids are known as **Queens**.

Knights are masculine spirits. They are the quiet (if not silent) protectors of their homes and their bonded. They typically bond with men in particular or masculine people in general. Knights can form nearly impenetrable shields around whatever they wish to protect. Land-bonded knights are known as **Princes**.

Jacks are non-binary spirits. They do not have the offensive capabilities of the maid or the defensive capabilities of the knight, but they are competent in either area. Jacks are known for their unpredictability, and are known to bond with humans over something as seemingly insignificant as eye colour. Jacks prefer to bond with those whose identity lies outside the gender binary. A land-bonded Jack is known as a **Rogue**.

ABOUT THE AUTHOR

K. Henderson lives with her family in Kitchener, Ontario, Canada. She welcomes comments and questions via email at: khendersonauthor@yahoo.com *The Eldermaid* is her first published novel.